8-20-14 JE

THE GOOSE MOON

Whilst in Canada, Will Stryker kills a man in self-defence and escapes into the border snowline from the Mounties. He finds Linny Jule who's fleeing from her sadistic father. Deciding that his daughter has been taken from him, Larris Jule trails the pair south where he settles on Will's ranch as payback. Will confronts Jule and his gunmen in the midst of a mighty blizzard that engulfs the town. Can Linny rely on Will to do the right thing? And is the deadly pursuit finally over?

*Books by Caleb Rand
in the Linford Western Library:*

THE EVIL STAR
WOLF MEAT
YELLOW DOG
COLD GUNS

CALEB RAND

THE GOOSE MOON

Complete and Unabridged

LINFORD
Leicester

First published in Great Britain in 2005 by
Robert Hale Limited
London

First Linford Edition
published 2006
by arrangement with
Robert Hale Limited
London

The moral right of the author
has been asserted

British Library CIP Data

Rand, Caleb
    The goose moon.—Large print ed.—
Linford western library
1. Western stories
2. Large type books
I. Title
823.9'14 [F]

ISBN 1–84617–244–6

Published by
F. A. Thorpe (Publishing)
Anstey, Leicestershire

Set by Words & Graphics Ltd.
Anstey, Leicestershire
Printed and bound in Great Britain by
T. J. International Ltd., Padstow, Cornwall

This book is printed on acid-free paper

1

The Calgary Flyer

Will Stryker came in blind when Cale opened the pot for ten dollars and Brand followed. When all cards were down he picked up his hand and fanned it slowly. He was holding the seven, eight, nine and ten of spades. He closed the cards and thought about the odds of the six or the jack turning up, the chances of turning over the railroad gamblers.

Joel Beeker considered his choices then pushed his bet forward.

Cale and Brand took two cards each and Will called for one. Beeker placed a card in front of Will and frowned when it wasn't picked up, took a single card for himself.

Within moments, Cale was leading again. 'Twenty,' he said, with a wry smile.

Brand sneered, but followed on.

Without looking at the draw card, Will counted out the money, led Beeker in with his call.

Beeker hesitated, then equalled the bet. 'There's your twenty, an' fifty more,' he said.

Cale glanced at Will, then at Beeker. 'That's eighty you're in for,' he said. 'That's rough on us greenhorns.'

'But necessary,' Will muttered.

Cale shrugged, decided to stay in the game.

There was an oil lamp hanging from the ceiling of the caboose. Under its glow, Will looked confidently at the cards in his hand. 'I'm stayin' with these. They handle real well,' he said with a challenging smile, as he drew out his breed bull money. 'So well, I've got to back 'em up with a hundred more.'

'That's on the long side for me.' Brand dragged on his cigarette, pushed his chair away from the table.

Beeker chewed his bottom lip, clinked a big ring stone against his whiskey glass. 'That's nothin' more'n a bet from the table. It ain't foolin' me,' he said determinedly. 'If you want to stay in, it'll cost you *another* hundred.'

Cale looked from Beeker to Will and closed his hand, tossed the cards down in front of them. 'Too serious,' he said with a sigh.

Beeker glared at Will. 'Too serious for you, cowboy?' he asked harshly.

'No,' Will replied, his face deadpan. 'In fact, if you want to play on, it'll cost you another *three* hundred.'

Beeker chuckled, but with a little less confidence.

Will allowed himself a lean smile. He knew that Beeker had probably reached his cut-off point, the limit of the real value of his cards. Now, he'd have to make up the going. 'Them table stakes, is what *you* hide behind, not me,' he goaded. He looked out the narrow window of the caboose. Through the reflections of the poker group, the world, west of Medicine Hat appeared unimaginably black and featureless. 'I think it's called put-up or shut-up time,' he added calmly.

Cale spluttered and shook himself back to alertness. Brand whistled through his teeth and dropped the front legs of his chair back to the floor.

Beeker tugged at the collar of his shirt, had another look at the cards he held.

'I'm partial to your game, Stryker,' he said. 'But *I'm* supposed to be the one who gnaws hog. I got me a reputation to uphold.'

'You could lose more'n that,' Piper suggested to the travelling gambler.

'Yeah, if I was bluffin' or gamblin' even. But you fellers know I never do that.' Beeker stared coldly into Will's face, opened up his billfold and withdrew the seeing dollars. 'An' I'm puttin' up this lady an' her entourage to prove it,' he said, covering his bet with the queen, ten, eight, five and four of hearts.

Will guessed that Brand and Cale were working as Beeker's shills, knew that trouble was on the way when they traded nervous glances. A moment later, beads of sweat broke out on Beeker's face and he took a slug of his whiskey.

Will's right hand dropped below the table as his left covered his cards. One at a time he turned them over; the seven, eight, nine and ten of spades. He touched the fifth card which he'd played blind throughout, returned Beeker's troubled stare.

'I reckon he's got it. He's got the six,' Cale whispered.

Will raised a quizzical eye, then smiled enigmatically.

'No. *I* was holdin' that. It's the goddamn jack,' Brand said.

Will turned over the jack of spades. 'Some of us are just born lucky,' he said coolly.

The muscles in the gambler's face twitched, his chest heaved and he got to his feet. He kicked out at his chair, sent it crashing away from him. His face was contorted with anger, but he was working on his response. 'You know the odds o' playin' on that jack?' he accused. 'You been cheatin', you son-of-a-bitch.' He took a step back, rushed a hand inside his frock coat.

Cale shuffled away from lines of fire, and Brand issued some panicky curses as the enraged man drew out a gleaming belly gun.

Will shook his head. 'An' you just got your flush busted,' he sighed, as he brought up his right hand with the short-barrelled carbine he'd been cradling. The explosion reverberated wildly in the confines of the caboose, as Beeker's body slammed into a stack of market crates.

The gambler's hand dropped the belly gun and he blinked slowly, tried to form a word. He rocked forward with blood surging from the front of his fancy shirt. He dragged out a single step, and his upper body twitched in an ugly spasm. Then he fell across the table, his face staring lifeless into the pile of crushed dollars.

Will sat staring at him for a few seconds, then he got to his feet. He looked down grimly as he reaped his winnings. 'You were goin' to roll *me*. But I wouldn't have shot you for it,' he said.

With Cale and Brand watching him, he pushed the saddle gun into its leg holster. 'This really is for self protection,' he told them. 'I sat in this freeze-out to kill time, not any god-damn tinhorns. An' I ain't to blame for you two losin' hoss an' beaver, neither. But 'cause no law an' order agency's goin' to hear the truth if you're on the tellin' end, there's a change to my plan. I won't be stayin' on to Calgary.'

★　★　★

Leaning from the rear step of the caboose, Will could see the distant lights of Lethbridge. It was nearing midnight and the train was still rolling north, close to the Milk River trestle and Fort Mcleod.

7

The wind cut, and he held a wool mackinaw tight around his ribs. He groped for his travel sack, swung it across his shoulder and waited, stared into the wintry darkness.

Five minutes later the train jolted and slowed in its approach to the river bridge. When the whistle hooted and the brakes squealed, he said goodbye to the stove-warmth, gripped the hand rail and swung away from the wagon. With the bite of frozen rain across his face he swore, took a deep breath and let go.

He felt the crunch of the ground, tried to retain his balance. But his feet slipped and he fell into the deep slush that flanked the track. He was inches off the train's wheels, but he lay there stunned. Then the clatter quietened down and he saw the red tail lights of the caboose fading into the distance.

He lay still, listened to his rasping breath. The howl of the engine's whistle eddied back through the wind, then the only sound was the soft, steady hiss of sleet.

He thought about the forty or fifty miles south to the border, Flathead Pass and the next hundred on to Lonepine Lake and Polson, his hundred-acre spread. Buying the herd bull would have to wait. He had over a thousand dollars stuffed in his pocket, wouldn't have to dig halfway through a mountain to earn it.

Unsteadily he got to his feet. He was slick with mud and chilled to the bone, but he took a bearing on the track and moved off south, shuffled some because of the fall.

2

Came to Pass

Hidden behind a clump of wind-blown spruce, the crouching man peered through the storm. Something was moving, something dark that faltered, moved again and then was lost among the snowflakes that swirled down from Montana's Flathead Mountains.

For a moment the wind lulled, and the whiteness lifted to reveal a human figure waist deep in snow, struggling up the trail. The man pulled a glove from his right hand and slowly raised a short-barrelled carbine. He smiled thinly and squinted against the brightness, with a satisfied grunt rested his cheek against the cold stock.

'Can't be sure ... too far,' he muttered and lowered the gun.

The wind lashed past him with

renewed fury. He saw that the dark figure was still coming nearer and he raised the muzzle of the carbine again. He watched whoever it was stumble and fall, rise for another hesitating step, before pitching headlong into the snow.

Without leaving the shelter of the trees, the watcher looked back along the trail to where it curved and disappeared. But there was no other movement or sign of life. Nothing except the huddled, still figure who was already being mantled by snowflakes.

For a long moment he stood watching, then he worked his way slowly to the body. He dropped to his knees and swore quietly.

'I could've shot me a lady woman this time,' he said.

Under the falling snow he looked uncertainly about him, then he reached out and gently touched her chilled skin. He got to his feet, lifted the girl in his arms and, holding on to his carbine, he began a long struggle up the slope.

Back at the clump of spruce, he

stopped to tie-in his clothing. Then, pulling his collar up and his beaver cap down, he turned from the refuge of the forest to face the storm.

With many rest stops, it took the man more than an hour to fight the blizzard up the long slope. Near the top, a huge stony outcrop loomed before him, and he halted once again to catch his breath and rest his arms. Then he turned through a small clearing of jack pine and confronted a low, sod-roofed cabin. He stumbled forward, and kicked open the door, almost fell inside.

The light from one small window dimly lit a narrow rough-boarded cot, and he laid down the exhausted girl. Then he scooped up kindling to make them a fire in the cook stove. Along one side of the cabin, a bowed shelf carried some tins, star candles and half-empty bottles. The man groaned and shook his head.

'There's nothin' much good to man nor beast, here. Even keg drainin's would've done us *some* good.'

The fire brightened quickly and he placed on some blowdown and scraps of fresh wood. He walked over to the girl and loosened her heavy belted coat. Then he saw that her feet and ankles were wet, her skin boots dark and icy.

He removed his own mackinaw and held it in front of the stove until it picked up some warmth. He self-consciously tucked it around the girl, then sat before the fire and waited. He watched the melting snow drip from his fur cap and he closed his eyes.

The minutes passed and the storm hissed through the pine tops until a tired sigh from the cot broke into his thoughts.

Startled and uncomprehending, the girl fixed her eyes on the man. Then she looked about the cabin, and moved her arms beneath the big coat. She winced at the closeness of its pungent odour, and sat bolt upright. She might have leaped from the cot, but the man was quickly beside her.

'Take it easy, girl,' he cautioned.

'You're out o' danger now.'

'Where am I? What happened?'

'You got plumb tuckered in the snow. Lucky I found you an' brought you here.' The man smiled, took a step back. 'Did no one ever tell you about duckin' a border blizzard?'

'Yes, they told me.' The girl's voice, in spite of its fatigue, held a gritty resonance, and it brought a doubtful smile to the man's face.

He went to the long shelf and pulled down a few potatoes and an apple. 'Like most else, they're near froze,' he commented, and pulled a stubby-bladed knife from somewhere deep inside his clothing. Then he pulled off his cap, rolled up the sleeves of his woollen shirt and started to pare off thick peelings.

The girl still felt drowsy and couldn't do much more than watch him. She noted his short, fair hair and his bristly beard, the way his eyes incessantly flicked to the cabin window.

He turned to look at her. 'You want

14

some hot tater stew?' he asked.

The girl nodded. 'I thought tie cutters weren't starting until later in the spring,' she said.

'There's some start early to get the pick of the timber.'

'You're working for the company then?'

'I never said that, ma'am.'

'A *yes* or *no* would do,' the girl corrected, and swung her legs from the cot. She looked down at her stockinged feet. 'Where are my boots?'

The man nodded toward the stove. 'I hung 'em up to dry.'

'*You* took them off?'

'Well, the hook weren't big enough for all o' you,' he joshed. 'When they're dry you can put 'em back on.'

Suddenly it came to her that if it wasn't for this man, she'd probably be dead, a frozen lump beneath the drifting snow. 'I'm Linny Jule. You saved my life, and I'll never forget it,' she said impulsively. 'My pa's got a small ranch below Snowshoe Creek. So,

I'm acquainted with most folk round about here,' she added testingly.

Briefly the man stopped what he was doing and his face seemed to mask itself. 'You can call me Will,' he said, by way of a response.

'That's the same as your name then, is it?' she countered in her pernickety way. 'Will who?'

'Stryker. You know what I'm wonderin', Miss Jule?' he continued, reaching for the last potato.

'Yes. You're wondering why a girl would be idiotic enough to climb the pass on a day like this.'

'More, why *anybody'd* want to do it.'

'I was going to Kalispell.' Linny's small hands clenched. 'I'll be happy enough not seeing Snowshoe country again.'

'An' there's *someplace* I feel the same way about,' Will said, with quiet and genuine commiseration. 'Well, you're seein' my ugly mug for a few more hours yet, so why don't you turn in? We can talk some more tomorrow.'

16

Linny squeezed her eyes shut for a moment, then shook her head. 'No,' she said. 'I've done with sleeping for a while. I'd rather talk.'

Will started to build himself a cigarette. 'Then talk it is,' he agreed.

3

Shadow Jumper

Before dawn, twenty-five miles west of the snow-bound cabin, Larris Jule stirred from his sleep. He lay for a long time listening for sounds from the corral, but he heard nothing until first light when he rolled from his bed.

After a mug of strong coffee, he stepped into the clear, cool morning. There was a stiff breeze that tracked Snowshoe Creek and it raised fresh snow flakes in the waterside corral. The Overo paint mare was staring up at the close-timbered slopes of the Flatheads and paid little attention to Jule as he approached. For a while, the man stopped and watched, but the horse didn't face him, though it must have heard the clink of his spurs.

'Yep, sure is a shame to coop you up,

like this,' Jule muttered deceitfully. 'You want to be runnin' ahead o' that storm, don't you? Like the little bitch.'

He was angry when he stepped into the coral to rope the paint and get it snubbed. The horse was feisty and there was a film of sweat across Jule's face by the time he got the animal tied to the post. The paint wouldn't quieten and had the saddle off twice before Jule got it belly-strapped.

'I don't take to this any more'n you do,' he rasped. 'It's just somethin' that's got to be done. Now calm down, or you'll feel the wrong end of a rope as well.'

But the instant Jule loosed off the holding snap, the paint was away, ripping the lines from his grip. The horse moved hard and fast, snorted ferociously as it raced to the other end of the corral.

Cursing savagely, Jule stepped forward. But before he was within half-a-dozen paces of the animal, it broke wildly past him, its hoofs pounding the grit and dust. He made a grab for his rope, shook out a loop and advanced again.

The horse bared its big, yellow teeth, flattened its ears against its head. A shrill furious snort emitted from it and it broke again. It seemed to hurtle straight at Jule and the man had a swift, fearful vision of going under the flailing hoofs. But at the last instant the paint swerved, and, as it trampled past him, Jule dropped a loop over the animal's neck. The paint fought its way back to the snubbing post, but Jule managed to get it tied-in again.

Jule was breathing hard, realized it was no use trying to get any further until he'd calmed the horse. He edged closer, caught the halter and patted the horse's neck.

'Can't you get it into that bone head o' yours, I'm goin' to get you broke,' he told the paint, while continuing to stroke its deep, muscled neck. 'Why'd you keep fightin' me?'

The paint listened to Jule's patter

and quietened. It lifted a foot and pawed the ground and the wicked glint seemed to leave its eyes.

'You're a good learner; I just know it. You got the horse sense,' Jule said. But it was with a confidence he didn't feel and he kept running the palm of his hand along the paint's neck.

The horse was very still now. It breathed deep, lowered its head, no longer vigilant. Jule released the snap, and before the paint knew it, he'd sprung up into the saddle.

The horse whirled as it pulled away from the post. But Jule had a good seat, got both feet in the stirrups. For the shortest moment he was thrilled with his capture, then the horse kicked out its hind end and reared sharply. It twisted again, raised a great white snow flurry, but sticking like a burr to the saddle, Jule went along with it.

Abruptly the paint changed tactics. Its back arched and it began to stiff-leg across the corral. With each movement it seemed to go that much higher, come down that much harder. The shocks jarred Jule's spine and he felt the thrill turning again to anger.

It wasn't a question of hanging on to the ride any more. Each movement of the paint was agonizing and Jule's belly was full of pain. But it was the green-eyed anger that tore him up, busted him inside. He felt bile rise in his throat, knew he had no business on a horse that wanted to chin the moon.

4

Getting the Man

For a time Linny Jule sat silent, looking up at the darkening window. 'Tell me: are *all* men born brutal, or is it just *most* of them?' she asked eventually.

Will Stryker seemed to ponder the question. 'I guess there's *some*,' he said. 'Is that what you want to talk about?'

Linny looked up quickly. 'I don't know. I just wanted to get away.'

'An' you picked a blizzard to do it in?'

'There wasn't much snow down on the Creek. I thought I could make it easily.'

'You couldn't have waited a little longer?'

The girl hesitated. 'No. I've put up with enough . . . waited too long.'

'Hmm. Got to be somethin' to do with one o' those brutal men, you're so steamed up about. Is that what you're runnin' from?' Will continued to enquire.

'You're not one for tact are you, Mr Stryker?'

'You're the one who wanted to talk, missy,' he retorted.

'Yes, I'm sorry. There's someone I've seen . . . rather *haven't* seen for six months. Now he's coming back,' Linny answered evasively.

Will sucked on his cigarette, blew a pensive stream of smoke at the roof timbers. 'I get the picture,' he said. 'An' fryin' pans an' fires come to mind.'

'It's a cruel, violent man I'm running from. I haven't known much else since my ma died. Now I've had time to think, I — '

' . . . want out,' Will finished the sentence. 'I guess it's your pa you're talkin' about, but who's this feller who got you off on the salvation road?' he asked.

'If you've been long in border country, you'll most likely be acquainted with him. He's Ashley Cameron, a sergeant with the RCMP.'

Will gave a curious, ironic laugh and coughed on a mouthful of smoke. 'No. No, I ain't acquainted with him. But I know your story. I guess it's an old one. How does your mountie friend figure in all this?'

'He had trouble with Larris — that's my pa — last year. It was over wild horses for Fort Mcleod. That was Pa's fault. He lied to make money on his saddle-brokes. Ash was the police buyer and couldn't make a tally. He made Pa pay back. That was his job. But from then on, he wasn't allowed near our land.'

'Well, he wouldn't be, would he,' Will confirmed drily.

'No. It would have been for the best, if he had though. That's when Pa changed. He started taking out his frustration . . . his resentment, on me.'

'What happened to the mountie?'

25

'He wrote me. Last winter he was up in Calgary, but I didn't get to see him. The last letter was two months ago when he said he'd be here early in the spring. He was going to the new border barracks in Flagstone.' She looked out the snow-encrusted window. 'He's got to be out there now. How long do you think this snow will lie?' she asked suddenly.

Will laughed. 'I ain't for second guessin' a spring blizzard in this country. It may howl for a week. You should know better'n me.'

'Ash will bring more men out searching before a week's out.'

As if at the toll of trouble, Will flinched. Then he walked to the other side of the cabin and held a match to a coal-tar lamp. 'Yeah,' he said with concern, 'that's really somethin' to look forward to. But that trail you left's well covered. So it won't be before tomorrow. Now, get some more sleep, miss.'

★ ★ ★

It was still early morning when Linny opened her eyes. An ominous howling had begun in the hills to the north of the cabin. She knew it was the sound of a pack of hungry timber wolves. The storm had driven most game into hiding, drifted over the remains of the previous day's wolf kill. Now they were out for fresh game.

'How close are they?' Will asked.

'A mile or so.'

'Will they come this way?'

'Maybe. They know where there's meat on the hoof.'

Will picked up his carbine, levered a round into the chamber and cocked the hammer. He opened the door of the cabin and fired up into the heavy sky. The report of the gun made an enormous sound in the still landscape, echoed off the surrounding timberline three or four times before silence returned.

'That shut 'em up,' he claimed, and returned to the coffee he'd been boiling.

'Well it would, wouldn't it,' Linny said, with a slight, sarcastic smile. 'Is the snow melting?' she asked.

'Not so's you can get far. Certainly not to Kalispell.'

'Suppose they find me here with you?'

'It'll be no worse for you, than for me,' Will said with conviction. He breakfasted on his half of the apple then, lighting a cigarette, he stepped over to the window.

'Hell. It must've been the gunshot,' he said calmly. The he turned and walked quickly to the stove. He seized the poker, scraped out the wood coals on to the floor and tossed the remains of the coffee water over them. 'Too goddamn late,' he muttered over the hissing coals, and picked up his carbine again.

Anxiously, Linny looked past his shoulder. Far up the trail towards the pass, beyond the jack pine that surrounded the cabin, a muffled figure was approaching through the snow.

'What are you going to do?' she asked, taking in the severe, hunted look that had appeared on Will's face. 'You can't see who it is from here.'

'Yeah, somethin' of a dilemma. By the time I can, I'll have to shoot whoever it is. Reckon they've sent someone after me. They must know I headed for the pass.'

Linny reached out and touched Will's arm. 'I don't understand. Are you in trouble? Who's after you?'

Will turned, nearly pushed her away. 'The law. It's the law that wants me,' he said. 'You just stay down. Keep out of it.'

'What have you done? Where's that place you don't want to see again?' Linny asked with increasing anguish.

'I had to kill a man across the border. They're goin' to say it was murder. Well, it weren't,' Will snapped. 'So, now you know. If you keep quiet, this buzzard might stay on the trail an' leave us alone.'

Linny crouched against the cot,

wondered who was approaching the cabin. She got up slowly, edged her way closer to the window. 'I deserve a look. Let me see,' she said to Will. 'I'm in this, whether you like it or not.'

The man had got closer, was standing well inside the belt of pine. It was the unmistakable shape of the flat-brimmed hat, the low sunlight on his face, that forced a gasp from Linny.

She flung herself against Will, seized the carbine and fought to pull it away from him. 'That's Ash. He doesn't want *you*: he's looking for *me*,' she yelled.

'He doesn't know you're here. No. Somehow, your mountie's after *me*. I don't want to shoot up no more than I have to, miss. But if he comes in here . . . ' Will let the threat of his words trail off.

'He doesn't know you, does he?' Linny asked quickly.

'More'n likely there's a description out on me.'

'But he's never seen you?'

'I think I'd remember. Why'd you ask?'

'Because I know him, for heaven's sake. Do you think I'm going to help you kill him? If he comes here, I'll make out you're my husband. I'll *say* you've been up here cutting ties, and I came with you.'

Incredulously, Will looked at her. 'You'll tell your intended, that *I'm* your husband? You think that'll save me? You tell him that, he'll more'n likely take off the top o' my head before han'cuffin' me, you dolt.'

'He *wasn't* my intended. He was someone who listened. Someone I turned to for help. He'll be piqued maybe, nothing more. I haven't seen him for more than half a year. He'll go back. Then you can go. Please?'

'You still think that much of him?'

'Yes. He's not the one who's hurt me.'

Will saw the torment in her eyes and made a grab for her wrist. 'Remember, this is the only life I've got, an' I'm

31

goin' to protect it,' he said gravely.

Linny drew her hand away, looked back through the window. The mountie had come nearer. He stepped out of his heavy wet snow-shoes and removing a fur mitten he unflapped his holster and moved toward the cabin.

Will cursed, gently laid down the carbine and moved his hand to his Colt. 'Go. Go tell him the good news,' he said. 'I'll stay back here to see how he takes it.' Very slowly Will drew his Colt. 'You tell him to leave us alone. I'm hopin' he might understand.'

5

Saddle Broke

At the end of the corral, the paint heaved itself against the poles, sought to scrape Jule from the saddle. But Jule wanted no more and he threw himself to the ground. He went sprawling, got the bite of sour dirt in his nostrils. He was halfway back to his feet when the paint hit him. It was so sudden, so unexpected that he had no idea what had happened. He felt himself being barrelled along, and panic clogged his throat when he realized the horse had turned on him. He'd been close to the side of the corral though, and as the outraged paint came piling back, he rolled to safety beneath the bottom pole.

Trembling with fear and fury, Jule lurched up on his knees. His face was running with wet, but he didn't know if it was from blood or sweat. His right leg ached furiously and for a moment he thought it was broken. The paint smashed itself against the poles again, then it bent its thick neck, put its head between its front legs and bucked violently around the corral.

Jule swore his retaliation and got to his feet. He ran to his cabin and, still enraged with defeat and frustration, he returned thumbing bullets into the breech of a Winchester.

'I'll put some goddamn lead in your goddamn brain,' he screamed at the paint.

But the horse had stopped bucking. It stood in the middle of the corral with its wild head flung up as Jule lined up his shot. He knew he couldn't miss, but something made him hold his fire.

'No. This is the coward's way out,' he rasped.

Jule had realized there was nothing wrong with his belly now, no bile in his throat. It hadn't been the paint's muscle that had thrown him from the saddle, but his own fear.

'You want me to show I ain't afraid o' you,' he challenged. 'Is that it? Is that what you're after?'

Jule let the rifle fall from his hand. 'Damn you,' he cried at the paint. He slid between the poles into the corral. 'I'll be the last person you ever throw,' he threatened.

He ran straight to the paint and made a grab for the reins, but the horse whirled and galloped away. Cursing, Jule snatched his rope and started off in a determined circle. He got the horse cornered and dropped the loop over its neck, over-handed swiftly up to the panicky animal.

The paint reared up, pistoned its forelegs high in the air. But Jule got himself a good hold on the hackamore and stubbornly held on. The paint snorted its anger and swung away, but Jule went with it. He made a grab for the saddle horn, caught it and went up into the saddle. The horse squealed its fury, was pitching and lunging even before Jule hit the seat. The base of his spine hit the cantle and it cracked his teeth together. But he stayed on, caught up the lines and found the flapping stirrups with his boots.

The paint went into the full grip of its fury as it bucked savagely across the corral. Jule didn't think the animal could be so violent as it tried to rid him from its back.

Realizing that his defeat was coming up, Jule's anger renewed itself. 'There's a bullet waitin' for you when I hit the ground, you evil brute,' he screamed at the paint. 'So throw me.'

The paint aimed for the side of the corral, but Jule saw it coming and swung his leg out of the way. The horse smashed with insane fury against the poles and rebounded, almost hitting the snubbing post. Jule got his foot back in the stirrup, settled in the seat again and raked his spurs along the paint's flanks.

'Not yet,' he yelled. The paint squealed and reared up, and for a breathtaking instant hung there, then it came crashing down on its back. But Jule had sensed the move and kicked free of the stirrups. He was on the ground when the paint came down and on impulse he hung a leg back across the saddle. The paint righted itself and lunged up on its feet. It started to rear again and Jule dug hard with his heels and sawed on the lines. But this time the paint came down on its feet and started crow hopping.

'You still ain't lost me,' he screamed.

The wetness on Jule's face ran into his mouth, and now he thought it tasted like blood. Then it dawned on him that the jolts weren't so severe any more. The paint's fury seemed to have diminished. It sprung its cannons and went for another hop. But it was half-hearted and it brought up still. It spraddled its legs and heaved its foam-flecked shoulders.

Jule could hear the shrill whistle of the paint's breath. He lifted a hand to wipe sweat from his face, noticed it really was blood that was pouring from his nose.

★ ★ ★

It was nearly first dark on the same day when Jule opened his eyes. He rose fully clothed from his bed and went outside. He stared across the lake, through the clouds of early emerging stone flies that swarmed along the water's edge. His whole body ached and he was still tired. But he was better, sated from his breaking ride.

He tugged at the slouch-brim of his hat, walked slowly past the wrangler's lodge to the corral where the paint stood indolently. A malicious expression cut across his face and he stood and watched the horse, felt the closest he'd ever get to regret.

'I'll stay the bad one o' this outfit,' he sneered.

The paint turned its head and looked briefly at him. Then it averted its gaze and just stood there, no longer a proud,

38

untamed animal.

'I'll wager you wouldn't have put up much of a struggle against Linny,' Jule said bitterly. 'I reckon she'll go south, then east to Kalispell. She won't be dumb enough to take the pass. Tomorrow, we'll go get her back.'

6

Opportunity

Linny took a deep breath, flung back the cabin door and stepped into the cold bright light. The mountie raised his head and for a moment they held each other's eyes, then he smiled and strode forward. He wore an elk-skin parka, and his figure cast a long shadow across the snow.

'Linny,' he called, his voice raised in cheerful surprise. 'What are you doin' out here? I thought you'd be down at the creek.'

Linny shook her head. She wasn't sure what to say or when to say it.

'Six months that seems like years,' Ashley Cameron went on. He was up close and his eyes were searching her face for an explanation.

Linny knew she had to say

something, had to make him believe her story. Her mind rushed back to where in the cabin's gloom Will stood silently, his gun pointed through the doorway. 'I'm married Ash,' she said, her voice weak and faltering.

The mountie's mouth opened slightly and he nodded, gave a curious, weary smile. 'Yeah, well, six months is a long time. He's in there, is he, your husband?' he asked, a little dismayed.

Linny chewed her lip and nodded nervously. 'He's a tie cutter. We came up to make an early start. You know, get the pick of the timber. But we got ourselves snowed in, instead.'

'I guess I'd best say 'hello' then. Keep it neighbourly,' the mountie said, drawing his Webley revolver.

Linny thought about standing her ground, but she smiled weakly and moved aside.

Inside the gloomy cabin the two men faced each other. Linny said their names, watched as they looked warily into each other's eyes.

'You're a little south o' your line, Officer,' Will suggested.

'For unlawful deaths, we got arrangements with border authorities,' the mountie said, pushing his heavy gun back into his holster. 'An American killed a passenger aboard the Calgary Flyer. He jumped the train outside o' Lethbridge an' headed south. Two nights ago we had him tracked close to the Montana line.'

'I thought a Queen's yellowleg never lost his man,' Will said with a half smile.

The mountie looked at Will carefully. 'You thought right, mister,' he told him.

'Do you know where is he now?' Will asked.

'I was on my way to Flagstone an' decided to see if he'd got this far. I reckon he did,' the mountie replied, with his own give-and-take smile.

'What's he look like?' Will asked casually.

'He's big. Got short corn hair, like a labrador pup, apparently.'

'Could well've been me, Officer, if I

hadn't been here, workin' for the company,' Will said, riskily.

'This man's got himself a small brand, apparently,' the mountie furthered. 'Some sort o' skin tear. A scar that runs around the heel of his left hand. A keepsake that stays with you, I'd say.'

Linny had turned away, but she twisted round to see that Will had already balled both his hands into loose fists.

Will looked coolly out of the window. The sun had disappeared and heavy snow clouds were piling up again above the pass. 'It's poor weather to be on a manhunt,' he contemplated. 'If this blizzard caught him near the pass an' he didn't get holed up, your job's done. There's hungry wolves that'll have found your quarry by now.'

The mountie considered what Will had said, then looked at Linny. 'This snow's goin' to stop me gettin' back to Flagstone,' he said with anticipation.

'Then you'll stay with us,' was Will's

prompt and attempted welcome. 'Linny an me's havin' an early supper. It ain't much, but you're welcome.'

'I got some food,' The mountie said, and handed Linny a leather satchel. 'It'll help out. There's some cheese, dried moose meat an' some cakes in there.'

★ ★ ★

The remainder of the day dragged on interminably, it seemed, for the occupants of the cabin. Looming trouble skulked among them and hardly a pleasant word was uttered. Linny improvised with the meagre food supplies while the two men split wood. It wasn't long after dusk that Linny said she was turning in.

'Not much else to do,' Will suggested, but the mountie didn't respond.

They slept little in the night of continuing wind and storm. In the early hours it grew deep and bitterly cold and Will replenished the fire. By dawn it was snowing less wildly and Linny took a pail, said she'd find fresh water.

Will shivered and wrapped his mackinaw tight around him. 'If this break holds, you can make it up to Flagstone,' he commented from the window.

'There's one thing I got to see before I go though,' the mountie said.

'Yeah, I know it,' Will accepted. He turned his left hand to reveal the distinct crescent-shaped scar. With his right he went for his gun, but the mountie was ready and his hand was already into its grip on Will's forearm.

Will's finger squeezed the trigger as he struggled to free himself. The bullet took out the window glass and the mountie brought Will's wrist down hard against his knee. The gun flew across the room beneath the cot and the two men grappled desperately to get free of each other.

Will stooped, and lifting the mountie almost off his feet, he heaved him away.

The man's head struck the edge of the cot as he fell, but he was up before Will could regain his Colt. Locked together again, they brawled across the floor. They crashed into the stove, knocked out the stack pipe and the cabin immediately started to fill with choking smoke.

Will turned and made a grab for his carbine, but the mountie was his match and again they closed. Gripping with all his might, Will reached the mountie's throat, but was kicked back. They drew apart, winded, each watching and waiting for an opening.

Then, closing his bloodshot eyes, and with his head down, Will charged. The mountie swayed to one side like a bullfighter, and Will struck the cabin wall. He went down, but straight off he got to his knees. But this time the mountie bested him. He'd found Will's Colt and held it out steadily before him.

'Stay down,' he warned his half-dazed adversary. 'I'll shoot you rather than take any more o' this.'

Then Linny pushed through the door. She sprang between them. 'Stop it,' she yelled, but the mountie warded her off.

'He's the man we're after, Linny. I knew it last night,' he said. 'He goes to Flagstone with me. Then back to Fort Mcleod for trial.'

'But he can't,' Linny protested, 'he's — '

'Whoever he is, Linny, he's *not* your husband,' the mountie butted in. 'I'd say you came up with that story just to stop him shootin' me when I came down the trail. And for that I'm grateful.'

'But you can't take him Ash. He saved *my* life.' Hurriedly, Linny told how the man named Will Stryker had found her in the snow and brought her to the cabin. 'He didn't have to. He could have gone on.'

'I'll remember to mention it at the trial,' the mountie said sharply. 'He's a killer an' I'm authorized to take him back. Law-abidin' folk wouldn't want it any other way.'

'Yes, I know that, Ash. But do you really think he would have killed a good man? There has to be an alternative price to pay. You're a sergeant, can't you use initiative?'

The mountie shook his head. 'None o' that figures in the police manual,' he said, standing in the open doorway, looking east where some shine was piercing grey clouds over the Flatheads. He turned around and tossed the Colt for Will to catch, then with a motion of his hand, indicated that he get to his feet and take the carbine. 'I'm not goin' to ask your name, mister, 'cause I never met you. But you'll find I can be a real unforgivin' whoreson if you ever set foot in Canada again,' was his ultimatum.

Will was already into his mackinaw, was reaching for his beaver cap. 'I ain't a complete fool, Sergeant,' he said, breathless and grateful.

On the edge of the pine belt, Will

stopped and looked back to where Linny now stood in the doorway. 'Kalispell,' he called out. 'Maybe we'll meet there.'

7

Dog Hole

At the north end of Lonepine Lake, Kalispell sat on a flat stretch of irrigable land. In the water blue of dusk, a sheltered bridge took Will Stryker across the Stillwater River to the logging camp at the outskirts of the town. Further on, two-storey buildings stood off from each other, hugger-mugger either side of a wide, dirt thoroughfare. Behind them, log on stone houses squatted next to tent frames. Five miles to the east of the town, the road met an aspen-lined gully. Then it bent around the lake, got cloaked in the foothills of the Mission Range whose deep shadows formed hard upon the town.

Will calm-talked his ten-dollar montana mule as he rode. He looked at yellow lights that bloomed in open doorways, tried to see through windows that were coated with dust. He walked on past sporadic cheering and thumping of bar-room pianos, glanced down dark alleyways where fierce-eyed men wandered.

The street was still busy, and most people seemed to be on the verge of being ridden down or driven over, as they weaved among wagons and horse-men.

Halfway, at the maw of one of the shadowy side streets, Will saw an old man sitting in a rocker.

'Good place to see a lot,' he said, while eying the broken bottles and torn playing cards that littered the nearby ground.

'Yep, just about everythin'. I know more'n I ever tell though. An' I ain't sided up, either.'

'How do you mean?' Will asked him.

'Sided up on one side or the other,' said the old man crabbily. 'I'm so old, nobody cares where I am. They reckon

I'm sittin' here waitin' for rigor to set in. You sided up, stranger?'

'No,' Will said and moved off. He heard the old man's cackle, wondered how long it would be, before he found out exactly what was meant.

He reached an intersection, where a hotel, a hardware store, and two high-fronted saloons faced each other crossways. One was the Red Pepper House, the other's faded sign said, 'Buckwoods'. Beyond that was a lane that led to a stable into which he turned.

The dark ground was stinking damp and covered in horse droppings.

'Gettin' hung in Fort Mcleod don't seem such a bad thing,' he muttered, patting the neck of his mule.

At the end of the rank alley, a man drifted out of the stable's darkness and looked closely at him. 'Second stall back,' he said.

Will gave the mule a small drink at the yard trough, removed its gear to hang up. For a moment he stood in the stall, his hand lying on the gummy sweat of the animal's back. He turned and looked into the blue eyes of the Overo paint mare in the next stall, then walked to the street. His mouth was parched and he leaned into the drinking trough, sucked at the water until he was near full.

Buckwoods had a swinging door with a window in it made of tinted glass. The saloon lights shone through yellow and red and blue, gave customers' faces rainbow colours as they entered.

There was a card game going on inside. Four men sat under a deep cloud of smoke with the bartender standing by. But that was all, because it was supper hour and slack time. Will stood at the bar and took his whiskey quick and returned to the street. He stopped for a smoke he had no need of, but it served to cover his inactivity as the town got primed for nightfall.

★　★　★

There was going to be trouble in the Red Pepper House that night. The proprietor knew it as he eyed the man who was considering his cards against the faro dealers.

For an hour, Larris Jule had played recklessly. He'd won and won again, could do no wrong. Then his luck changed and he started to lose. Each time he lost, he took huge gulps of whiskey and muttered dire threats. Eventually his anger erupted and he cursed loudly and flung his drink across the room. The shot glass bounced once then skidded along the floor before hitting the sleeping dog in its soft underbelly.

Not understanding, the dog flattened its jewels against the floor and snarled a warning.

'Steady, Rio,' Hyram Hollister, its owner said uneasily. 'He didn't mean it. He's drunk.'

Jule's face twisted with unpleasantness. 'Don't growl at me, you stinkin' cur,' he spluttered. He staggered towards the dog and made a threatening poke with his foot.

'Leave him alone,' said Hollister, 'you're frightenin' him.'

The dog bared its fangs, gave a low defensive growl and stood with its hackles raised. For his answer, Jule raised his foot and kicked the dog hard in its ribs.

'No! Rio, come back here,' the dog's owner called.

But Rio wasn't going to get back unscathed. Jule's hand moved quickly to his belt. He pulled his gun and fired a shot down into the floor. It was cruelly close to Rio and he yelped in distress.

'Well, you won't be aimin' to bite no one else,' Jule sneered. 'The only thing wild animals understand is a length o' rope or a bullet.'

Larris Jule's act of congenital nastiness took Hollister's breath away. The dog was his constant companion, had been his 'pard' while he'd trapped beaver and fox in the frozen waste of the Missions.

His eyes blazing, Hollister picked up a half-empty whiskey bottle from the table and flung it close to Jule's head. 'He weren't goin' to bite. You scared him,' he said, his voice low and trembling with emotion. 'I'll kill you for that, you pig.'

The others in the saloon held their breath. They saw the instability in Larris Jule's eyes, heard the tyranny in his slurred voice.

'The hell you will, dog boy.' Jule took a step forward with his arms outstretched. But Hollister made a fast sideways movement and Jule stumbled, went down to the floor beyond him. With a howl of rage the man regained his feet, wiped away a smudge of blood from his gashed lip.

Hollister was standing a few paces away. He was taking steady, deep breaths, waiting for Jule's next onslaught. He was pale-faced, but reckoning, as he swayed backwards and forwards on the balls of his feet.

Jule grinned in roostered fury, feinted

then rushed. But Hollister avoided him again, got home a straight left into Jule's body. Jule gasped and doubled up, then with a roar, bored in with his head down. Hollister caught him twice on the head, but nothing was going to stop the man. Hollister stepped back while hitting out in desperation, got home another blow. But still Jule came on, racked with brutish torment.

Jule cursed, flung himself at Hollister. But the trapper evaded him and with a quick movement edged round the table.

Jule seized the table and flung it behind him. Behind Hollister now there was a wall and he had no escape. Jule gave a thin wintry smile and charged forward, closed his arms around Hollister's upper body. Bear-like, Jule squeezed and swung Hollister off his feet, swung him violently to one side.

Hollister clattered down, threw up an arm as he cracked the side of his temple against a table leg. Then he lay unmoving, his body twisted ominously into the puncheoned floor.

Two men detached themselves from the small crowd. One of them turned Hollister's body over so that they could see his face.

'He ain't breathin'. You've hurt him real bad, mister,' the man said.

The others had fearful glances at the body, then slunk away when the Pepper House proprietor stepped forward.

'I saw what happened,' he said. 'Poor Hyram. Who'll take care o' that dog now?'

Larris Jule draped his coat over his shoulders, pulled on his hat and walked over to where Hollister lay. A malicious expression cut across his face.

'He shouldn't have got involved, an' I got nothin' to answer to,' he told the men around him.

'Well, ain't that neat,' a man who was standing near the door remarked.

Jule looked at the man and sucked in air through his teeth, but said nothing.

The man moved aside. He looked into Jule's eyes, saw the fear that bullies carry with them.

'Who was *he*?' Will Stryker asked, when Jule had gone.

'Don't know much about him, other than he's a nasty piece o' work. He mentioned Whitefish, but I don't know if that's where he's from,' the saloon owner said. 'He told someone he's here lookin' for his daughter.'

'Whitefish, eh,' Will said half interested. Whitefish was an *en-route* town, east of the Flatheads, along the Stillwater. It was where he'd bought the mule, got another six inches cut from the barrel of his carbine the mountie from Fort Mcleod had returned to him.

'I'll wager she ain't lookin' for *him*,' the saloon boss offered up as an afterthought.

'About the dog,' Will reminded him. 'It's a coonhound, an' I'll take care of it.'

8

Trespass

As he rode, Will thought of Linny Jule, remembered how he hadn't had the time or inclination to tell her about Kalispell. On his way back from the cabin in the Flatheads, the town was never going to be more than a stop-over for him. His own small outfit was eighty miles further south, at the other end of Lonepine Lake.

His hundred acres were hidden in the hills, miles from any established trails. In the five years he'd owned the ranch, he'd only ever kept a small herd. He worked the land alone, but every fall, hired two or three punchers for the drive down to Missoula. He made enough to live comfortably, made extra by wolfing and washing gold in the headwaters of the Swan River.

Now, two days' ride from Kalispell he was near froze, but nearly home. He came out from a stand of pine, watched his cabin for a full minute before he swore. He held the reins tight, told the hound to 'stay' and 'keep quiet', even though it hadn't made a sound.

There were five horses in his corral, and smoke from the chimney of his cabin was rising grey and thick into the leaden sky. He sat the mule, watched stunned as a rider led a claybank horse across the yard in front of the cabin. Then he smiled bleakly, swore and drew the mule back towards the timber. He knew with absolute certainty that whoever was down there had spotted him.

Holding the barrel of his carbine under his mackinaw he worked his way to a new vantage point. It was off the trail, where snow-covered ridges of rock cut into the timberline. He was deeply shaded by the approaching night, and he paused for a full minute to listen before working his way forward through the trees. He 'shushed' the hound, indicated that it lie flat. The dog was alert, its nostrils twitching. Its senses reached into the night, tested the air for what it held.

But the soft, dark silence closed in again, and he decided to move. He walked on, cautiously rounded another ridge and saw the claybank. It was standing with its head down, partly sheltered by the rocky overhang, as it waited.

He'd been right then; somebody was coming for him, and they were close. He stood hard against a sentinel pine, his body merging with the blackness of the trunk. It was dark now and no bird or rabbit moved. They were wise, like most snowline critters, knew when to seek shelter.

Will's fingers started to ache with the cold, and he flexed his grip on the carbine. The carpet of white sparkled under the indigo darkness, but he found it hard to keep tabs on the claybank as it moved against the rock face. He heard it shift its feet, and then saw the saddle as its wet leather glistened.

Then there was something else. A sharper sound as a boot scuffed on loose stone. Carefully Will lifted the carbine and crooked its short barrel in his left hand. As the man silently took up the reins of his horse, Will spoke.

'You found me, mister, an' you been on my land long enough.'

In one smooth movement the man went into a crouch and twisted his body. There was a stab of fire out of the blackness, and the crash smothered the sound of Will's own carbine. He felt the smack of the bullet as it hit the tree beside him; that close he even smelled the resinous tang of wounded bark.

Realizing the other man was no regular cowpoke or horse wrangler, Will fired again, twice in quick succession. He heard an ominous dull thud, stared into the darkness at what he thought was the man's body crumpling into the drifting snow. He edged back around the pine, took a deep breath and kept very still.

He wasn't about to close in on a man who hadn't cried out at being hit. The claybank turned to search out Will. It was spooked at the gunsmoke and blew hard from its fleshy nostrils.

A cold, curling wind stirred Will's mackinaw and he shivered, called gently for the hound. 'Come here, Rio,' he said, and held down the fingers of his left hand for contact.

He was looking almost directly at the dark shape of the man when the next shot came. As the bullet tugged sharply at his coat, Will fired. He was momentarily blinded by the flash, but it was the guiding light, and all he needed was the one accurate shot.

'Go take a look,' he said, and the hound moved stealthily forward.

Will was in no mood to make a move, and he levered another round into the carbine. As he calmed, anger took over. Mostly because he didn't know who he'd set about killing or why. In the years since he'd got his land, there'd been fewer than a handful of visitors. Now, all of a sudden he'd been taken over and was being shot at for speaking his mind.

'Goddamn it,' he said as a sudden thought struck him. 'Out of the way,' he warned the hound as he moved forward. He pointed the barrel of the carbine down at the man's head. 'You ain't related to that railroad tinhorn who tried to stiff me, are you? That's the only trouble I been in lately.' But Will knew he wasn't, that he was stone dead.

Near the man's outflung hand, he saw the glint of a Colt. Pushing the tip of his gun barrel hard into the side of the man's face, he prodded with his toe. He rolled the body, upturned the face to the gently swirling snowflakes. 'Jesus, he ain't much beyond majority.' Will looked hard at the man's gunbelt. 'An' he ain't ever made a dollar from the saddle,' he suggested.

Will lifted the body and heaved it up and over the claybank's saddle. Then he picked the man's Colt from the snow. 'A Remington, but this *ain't* a brand I know,' he said, slapping the horse's flank gently. 'Reckon it'll go back to where it gets fed. That's where I'll find it.' He stood back and watched the horse move off down the trail, the bulk of the dead man draped across the saddle.

There was moonlight now, and Will stepped up to the point of the ridge. He pulled the collar of his coat tight around his neck and peered through the falling snow. The door to his cabin was open and a wedge of thin yellow light fell across the front of his corral. There was still some distance between them, but he thought he recognized a paint mare. It was sniffing the air, pawing the slush, watchful and impatient.

'Who the hell rides you?' he wondered moodily.

As a town, Polson wasn't much of a size or style. There was a hotch-potch of single and double-storey dwellings that faced each other across a broad street, a livestock pen, livery stable and two or three stores. It supported one lodging house and two saloons. One had a sign that said nothing more than, Beers and Spirits. The other was called Sentence Hotel, because the owner sometimes pitched a drunk customer into a sleeping shed that ran along the back.

It was just short of midday when Will rode in. He tied his mule at the hitching rack and stepped up to where a wide door had replaced the batwings. Rio had a look about and decided not to go in.

Two of the men at the bar were strangers, the third was Circuit Sheriff Abe Dancer. The fourth was called Buckham Sendaro, a fur trapper from the Missions.

'Didn't figure on seen' you around this late in the year, Will,' Abe Dancer said.

'Sorry to disappoint you, Sheriff.' Will wasn't going to say any more. Since he'd last spoken to Dancer, he'd killed two men. So talking trouble didn't seem the thing to do. Besides, Sheriff Dancer was doing his own thinking. As far as he was concerned, Polson was the end of the line in more ways than one. He was married now and father of a little boy, and he wanted no trouble. But he couldn't help but wonder what had brought Will Stryker down from the hills.

'Mail wagon's about due,' he commented, still wondering.

Will grinned. 'Nothin' much changes around here, does it?' he said jokily.

There was a curious, dark silence for a few minutes, until a raised voice issued from the street.

'We got a passenger, Sheriff.'

Sendaro moved over to the door and looked through the snow-frosted glass. 'Yep,' he said. 'There's a passenger out there all right. Don't look like he's goin' any further.'

Everyone moved to see the day's interest. But Will refilled his glass.

Sendaro glanced at him. 'You ain't the enquirin' sort, are you, Will?' he said.

'I've seen dead men. Most of 'em have been fairly cold.' Will swallowed his drink and turned towards the opened door. The two strangers came in carrying a body between them. They looked around, then uncaringly laid it out on the floor. Abe Dancer returned with a man who was obviously the wagon driver.

'About seven, maybe eight miles out,' he was saying. 'I come round a bend and there was this sodden claybank totin' the stiff. I figured it was headed this way . . . somethin' for you, Sheriff.'

Dancer stared disagreeably at the dead man. Why didn't they let the goddamn horse keep going? he thought. 'Anybody know him?' he asked, but the heavy silence returned. Sendaro glanced quizzically at Will, and Dancer noticed it.

'He's been shot up some,' the driver said. 'I'd say from early last night.'

At Dancer's sharp glance, the man flushed up a little. 'I used to drive an ambulance for the infirmary at Billings,' he said. 'I can always tell you, how long.'

'Hmm. In this weather, the horse probably hadn't come that far,' Dancer said.

Will had a guess at what the sheriff was thinking. He knew there weren't too many places the dead man could have come from; not if his horse had joined the wagon road west of Polson.

'Well, he weren't backshot,' Will remarked dispassionately.

'That ain't surprisin',' Sendaro said. 'This boy's Slender Madge, an' he don't make his livin' pullin' meat from traps.'

'So *that's* Slender Madge, is it?' Dancer said. 'I wonder what he's doin' in these parts. He's a young gunny an' wanted for murder.'

Will swore under his breath. He was right about the man who attempted to kill him not being a ranch worker. 'Yeah, can happen to the best of us,' he murmured and looked to Sendaro.

'Who do them animals belong to outside? That knob-head yours, Will?' the trapper asked as if to break Dancer's train of thought.

'Yeah, an' the red tick. Just be careful what you say about him. I stopped just short o' killin' the last man who upset him.'

Sendaro raised an eyebrow. 'I'll bear it in mind,' he said appreciatively.

'I wonder who this owl was workin' for?' Will said, trying to hide the anticipation.

'If he used the stable, old Caddo might be able to tell us who's payin' the bill,' Dancer said.

The sheriff knew that even if he discovered something from the livery man, he'd more than likely keep quiet about it. It was part of the non-involvement pact he'd made with himself.

Will knew it too, knew he'd have to go and speak to the old man himself.

9

Second Encounter

A drafty, not so long-standing structure lay at one end of Polson's broad street. Outside, a lantern hung over a barely legible sign that designated it the livery stable. In front was a windowless little room in which a stove glowed cherry-red.

'Hay's for the takin' an' there's grain if you've a mind. But that'll be four bits extra,' a voice crackled out of the gloom.

'That's a price to pay,' Will offered in return.

'Take it or leave it, mister. But you so much as stick a finger in my corn bin without payin' an' I got somethin' here that'll open your belly from the back.'

'I got me a mule outside . . . dog, too. If you give me what I want, an' tend to 'em, I won't burn this place down around you. You hear me, you decrepit old goat?'

'I hear. Is that you, Will Stryker?' Caddo demanded.

'Yeah, it's me. Out o' season, I know, but it's me.'

'You should've said straight off,' Caddo said. He appeared swathed in a fur robe, under a felt hat had a scarf wrapped tight around his ears. He lowered the barrel of his scattergun and screwed up his face. 'What is it you're after?' he asked, not missing Will's bespoke sidearm.

'I want to know about a group o' men. One of 'em was no more'n a kid. He carried a leg-strapped .44 Remington an' rode a claybank. Gunfighter, some say. You remember 'em?'

'Yep, I remember 'em. They rode in a couple o' days ago. One of 'em weren't goin' to pay for grain. He was a mean son-of-a bitch.'

'Ridin' a paint was he, this mean son-of-a-bitch?' Will asked.

'Yep, an' he took my piggin' buckboard. Gave me a dollar for the use of. Can't think of what for. It's tied up back o' the lodgin'.'

'Thanks, Caddo,' Will said. 'How much you charge for lettin' me sleep in the lean-to?'

'Hee, hee. I should be payin' *you* to go in there.'

Will smiled. 'Why, ain't it got a cot?'

'It ain't hardly got a roof, but you're welcome,' the old livery man guffawed.

After seeing that his mule was tended to, Will got himself an icy sluice from the trough. Then he thought he'd get some hot food at the hotel, maybe wheedle some meat for Rio. If he got lucky, he'd be killing three birds with one stone.

There were few sidewalks in Polson and Will trod the drifting snow between the scattered buildings. He didn't go straight to the hotel, thought he'd bend around, get a look at Caddo's buckboard.

Maybe it was luck, maybe something

else, but as he got close, the back door of the lodging house opened. A slight figure came out and looked across the town, turned towards Will as he approached. His mouth worked silently and then he gulped. He was taken by surprise and fixed for something to say.

On the slight rise of the steps, Linny Jule was caught the same way. But she was more ready, was the first to overcome it. 'Will,' she said, uncomfortable surprise edging the pleasure. 'What are you doing here?'

'This is my home town. Well, the town that's nearest my home. It's where the trouble is,' he added, foreseeing a smile from Linny. 'There's a passel o' jayhawkers staked out at my ranch. I don't know what it is they want, but I'm catchin' up with 'em. They've been stabled here in town.' Will shrugged and irritatedly pulled the skin cap from his head. 'Still, that ain't nothin' to do with you, Linny,' he said. 'Anyways, I thought it was Kalispell you were headed for. You still runnin'?'

Linny knew there was no sense in stalling, putting together a story. 'Yes, I am still running, Will. And all this *is* to do with me,' she said.

'How'd you mean?' Will asked, with a quizzical shake of his head.

'It's my pa, that's up at your ranch,' she said, discomfited but direct. 'I thought the place belonged to a horse scout. I didn't know what was going on, until I saw something with your name on it.'

Will took a step forward, his face now chewed with deep confusion. 'Your pa . . . you didn't know . . . what the hell?' he hemmed and hawed.

A bloodless mark showed along Linny's bottom lip, where she'd bit hard. 'Please believe me, Will. It was Ashley Cameron. He told Pa of you and me at the cabin in the Flatheads,' she said. 'He made heaps of it . . . thinks that you took something that was his . . . something that *belonged* to him.'

'Sorry, Linny, but your pa must be some backward son-of-a-bitch. You ain't one of his chattels.'

Linny gave a feeble smile. 'I tried to reason with him,' she said. 'I told him the truth . . . what really happened, but he didn't believe me. He won't see any sense. Now he wants to take away from you . . . take something that's *yours*.'

'You told him my name an' he followed me all the way here for that?'

'No.' Linny shook her head sadly. 'He followed me to Kalispell, because I'm his *daughter*. *You* were the excuse. He always thought that possessions were cheap . . . there for the taking. Lives too, sometimes.'

'Well, my piece o' land an' my house might be cheap, but they certainly ain't there for the takin'. It's my home,' Will assured her, bluntly.

'What are you going to do?' she asked, slow and fearful.

Will took a moment to answer. 'Don't know yet,' he said. 'But gettin' back what's mine seems reasonable.'

'I can try again. Make him listen to sense. I'll have to stand by him. For a while anyway.'

'If he's aimin' to stay on my land, it won't make sense to stand in *front* of him,' Will said with explicable anger.

Linny's dread increased. 'He brought some men with him. They'll be there,' she said.

'Not quite all of 'em. Your pa sent out a welcomin' party. He needs their help to get you back to Snowshoe, does he?'

'No. They're mustang runners. He would have found wild horses and herded them back. He saddle-breaks them for the RCMP.'

'Yeah, I remember, you told me,' Will said, with a bleak smile. 'So if you stay, his sojourn won't be a total waste o' time.'

'It's how he sees it. It's another reason for what he's done.'

'Give me credit for not understandin', Linny, but right now, your pa an' his men have got their boots under my table. So *reason* don't figure with me.'

'Promise me you'll go talk to him, before you start shooting.'

'Well it ain't goin' to be a duel, Linny. For someone so off beam . . . so pig-headed, he ain't goin' to be easy to talk to. But I'll try. By the way,' he added, 'there's a paint mare in my corral that I think I've seen before. You know it?'

Linny was taken aback. 'Yes,' she said, 'I think I do. She wasn't saddle broke when I last saw her, though. I guess Pa must have thrown more than a loop at her.'

Will looked outraged as he considered what Linny was saying. 'Has he raised a hand to you again?' he asked.

'No. For a while, he'll be content with just getting me back.'

'You takin' the buggy out there?'

'Yes, I just told you. Circling the timber, it's two hours ride. I want to be there before dark.'

'I *know* how far it is, Linny,' Will retorted, his voice short and sour. 'You tell your pa that this time I ain't turnin' around. Not on my own land. Tell him he'll have to find someone better'n Slender Madge. He'll understand.'

10

Pursued

Up on the snow-swept ridge, Will had waited until Larris Jule's henchmen had ridden from his ranch before he made a move. He was hoping that Linny would have a serious go at negotiating on his behalf. Tell her pa that he'd got it wrong, that Will Stryker was a gentleman, and that he should have his cabin and land back.

And an apology would be fine, Will thought scornfully. He swore and heeled the mule forward, told Rio to leave the pretty, winter-coated rabbits alone. He approached his cabin from the east, through a deep scoop under the trees, where he was screened by the drifting snow. The hound stayed off, keeping to the higher ground where the footing was more firm.

When he came into the open he saw the buggy that Jule had hired for Linny. In the poled corral, the Overo paint turned and looked ruefully at him. Then it cast a blue eye on Rio, and Will remembered where he'd seen it before. It was in the next stall to where he'd stabled his mule at Kalispell.

He wasn't going to get close up to the cabin because the paint decided to sound its unease. He leaned forward in the saddle, pulled kindly at one of the mule's ears. He'd wait, stay hidden until Linny's pa stepped on to the narrow stoop.

Larris Jule had wondered about the disturbed horse and, in less than a minute, he emerged cautiously from the cabin. But the paint was settling, and there was no noise except a fractious snort, and Will levering the action of his carbine.

A magpie rose from the trees and Larris Jule's jaw dropped. He whirled to face the sound of the mechanism

81

that grated sharp across the snowy clearing.

'I'm Will Stryker, an' I want you off my land,' Will called to him clearly. 'Killin' ain't what I'm after, so I'm hopin' you'll think wisely about it.'

Jule held a Winchester at his side, had its barrel point to the ground. 'Have we met before?' he asked. 'I don't remember.'

'Hardly *met*. It was up in Kalispell. There was a red tick coon hound. His owner died tryin' to protect him. Perhaps you remember *that*,' Will retorted.

Jule's wary eyes narrowed as he recalled the event.

'An' you know what I'm thinkin' now, *Mister* Jule?' Will persisted. 'I'm thinkin', what's a coon hound, an Overo paint an' your daughter got to share? Why, I'll tell you,' he said before Jule had time to think. 'They all get to be bullied an' beat by a thievin', cowardly snipe-gut.'

Will could see the anguish as the man

turned to face his daughter who'd come into sight from the cabin.

Jule made to spit in the snow at his feet, but he didn't take his eyes off Will. 'As for *your* land, there's some folk in Polson reckon this place was abandoned. So I reckon I got *me* a claim an' *you'll* be startin' over,' he said spitefully.

Will almost smiled. 'I told Linny I wasn't leavin' this piece o' land again.'

Jule *did* smile. 'Then you told her wrong.'

'You know I can take you, Jule. You're relyin' on Linny bein' here to stop me.'

'No. I'm relyin' on my men,' Jule retained his stinging smile. 'You think I'd send 'em into town knowin' you were comin' back?'

Will had a hard, accusing look at Linny, as Jule continued, 'They should be turnin' back over the ridge about now. One of 'em's Madge's uncle. *He'll* be real pleased to see you.'

Linny jumped from the stoop. 'Get away, Will. He's serious mad an' he'll see you dead. Please go,' she pleaded.

Will heeled the mule a couple of steps towards Jule and Rio followed close. 'I've done nothin' to harm you. But from now on, I'm takin' the benefit of this bein' a godforsaken an' lawless territory,' he said with quiet menace.

'Meanin'?' Jule sneered.

'I've changed my mind about not wantin' to kill. I'm goin' to take you one by one,' Will vowed.

Jule made a hostile sound from deep in his throat, violently swung up his Winchester. The coon hound blinked its inquisitive eyes, then it pulled its mouth tight around its fangs and snarled.

Jule went to move off the stoop, but Will had guessed at his intention. He quickly dismounted before warning him. 'You raise a finger to that dog, mister, an' so help me, I'll cut it off an' give it him to piss on.'

As Jule pulled back the hammer of his rifle, Linny reached out quickly and grabbed Will's coat sleeve. 'No!' she cried, and tugged him off balance as her pa's rifle crashed out.

The bullet whined across the snow-scape, narrowly missing Will's neck and the mule. He swore and reached down with his right hand to pull the cut-down carbine from its scabbard.

Jule fired again. But he was strung up and worried for fear of hitting Linny. Will's bullet slammed high across his shoulder, knocked him hard against the wall of the cabin. He dropped to his knees and the rifle fell from his fingers. He was reaching for it with his left hand when Will fired again. But it was a shot for scaring, not killing. Will couldn't bring himself to do that, not with Linny watching.

He stood and watched, uncertain what to do next. Linny, too, was in doubt, and also frightened. She went back on to the stoop and hurled her pa's Winchester out into the snow.

'Please go, Will. They'll be here any minute. One of them *is* Madge's uncle,' she called out. Then she helped her injured pa back into the cabin.

The mule was stompy now, bothered by the gunshots and the squealing from the paint in the corral. It was a wild few seconds before Will could get a foot in the stirrup and swing to the saddle. He gave a sharp whistle for Rio and kicked the mule into its eccentric run.

'I'll be back, Jule, I'll have me some final proof,' he gave as loud notice to her father. 'Linny, return that buggy to Polson, an' stay there,' he added.

★ ★ ★

Will headed west, toward Polson, but less than ten minutes later, when the mule swung up on a slight rise, the first gunshot cracked the cold air.

'Goddamn it,' he yelled. Jule was right. There were four horsemen between him and the ridge. He'd never make it that way. He pulled the mule around hard and headed north-east.

There was another gunshot as he headed for the rising ground at the head of Box Canyon. The mule was driving its legs through the snow. It was running all out, but Will didn't know how much it could take. Behind him, Jule's men were spanned heel to heel, riding wide of the cabin. Will galloped the mule for the timberline and Rio compassed them, enjoyed the adventure of soft snow around its legs.

It would be ill-fated for a bullet to find its mark at that range, but still, Will bent low at the occasional ranging shots from his pursuers. With the timber-covered slopes of the Missions looming and with the chill starting to gnaw at his body, he knew the riders had settled on out-running him.

Among the first of the rocky outcrops, Will reined in the mule beside a jack pine. He drew the carbine and sent off a rapid shot at the nearest rider. Then he fired another, then another as fast as he could lever shells into the breech and pull the trigger. With the wild gunfire crashing around him, he remounted and set off again at a run. The live-stock trader in Whitefish had assured him the mule was steady on its feet, a rimrocker, and Will decided to find out how much of one.

Another fifteen minutes hard ride and Box Canyon suddenly gaped wide before him. It was a quarter-mile wide at its easterly maw, but the only trail he knew of narrowed into a rocky cleft at the tail end of the canyon. Hoping there might be a chance on the north side, he ran the mule up the canyon for nearly a mile before putting it up a jagged bumpy slope. The mule sagged at the knees and snorted with exertion as it climbed. Will swung from the saddle on to the narrow defile and, gripping the reins, he hauled the animal upward, slipping and scrambling towards the top.

Somewhere close behind him, a bullet exploded against the rising wall of the canyon and fragments of rock splintered the flanks of his mule. Rio barked once, then lunged forward to head the way over the rim.

Sliding his carbine from its scabbard,

Will hunkered against a slab of wind-blown rock. He aimed carefully and triggered one shot into the four riders who were gathering on the canyon floor. A man shouted as he was hit, and Will sent another bullet down the narrow defile. A horse went down thrashing, and its rider scurried for cover. There was some return fire, but for the first time Will realized the shots were from revolvers; only one carried the distinctive crack of a rifle. He fired again, and knocked another rider from the saddle. The man fell, but his boot caught in the stirrup and the horse panicked and took off. It ran further up the canyon, dragging its rider, limp and insensible through the snow.

Will slowly got to his feet. True to his word he was taking them out one at a time. Larris Jule would be a jumpy, troubled man if he knew.

Despite the cold, Will was bathed in sweat and the mule was streaked with lather, and trembling. Will took the reins and walked slowly towards a stand of timber. He was in no immediate danger, the men below would be riding ahead for their stricken colleague. It would be another half-hour before they'd look for another way up. But they wouldn't rush it. Man or horse, one of them was out of action, and with skinless hands and face, the dragged man would be in little mood to fight. Will gave a thin, humourless smile and wondered if the man could be Slender Madge's uncle, if he could be the rifleman.

Will didn't leave much of a trail as steadily he moved further east. He held the palm of his hand down for Rio to rub his nose against and get reassured. Between his strip of land and the Missions, the country was wild and relatively unknown to him. He remounted, and a half-hour later found a spring that ran down from the peaks. He refilled his canteen and watered the mule, rubbed him down with handfuls of snow and soft pine fronds.

To the north, the mountains towered

high, and south, beyond Box Canyon, there were steep cliffs and deep gullies. Will's route lay further east, where the Post and Bole Creeks spilled their way towards the Missouri River.

If Larris Jule had the stomach for it, he'd be waiting for Will to return. Linny Jule, if she felt anything for her pa, would be offering up an entreaty. A plea to return to Snowshoe, with herself as the compliant and dutiful daughter. But Will was hoping she wouldn't. Being on the receiving end of a birch, wasn't a 'duty' to his way of thinking.

He rode on, but the terrain was harsh and the wind got colder. Several times he worried deer, and one time when he broke from cover of the pine, he saw a grizzly. From a hundred yards it watched him, stood on its hind legs for a better view until he'd ridden by.

Eventually, long, early-evening shadows crept down from the mountains, and the swirling wind even got to him through the trees. He mulled over his predicament and the mule twitched a responsive ear to his words. He handed down a strip of pemmican to Rio, thought it might cheer him up, take his mind off any racoons in the vicinity.

When darkness fell he swung down from the saddle, but he didn't stop. He walked steadily on, countering the mule's indignant tug on the bridle. The moon started its nightly climb and the land glowed unearthly bright under the canopy of stars. From a narrow shoulder of the mountain, the canyon dropped away. Snowflakes spiralled downwards hundreds of feet to a silver ribbon of creek. For a moment Will thought about the men who'd be following, then he waved Rio forward, started looking for suitable shelter where he'd make night camp.

11

Breaking Force

In a cleft of split rock, Will built his fire. The rock would reflect some heat, and he made a crude lean-to shelter of dead wood. He gathered snow to melt for coffee, preferring to keep what water he had in the canteen. With cold fingers he unwrapped the food packet that old Caddo had prepared for him, and then fed the mule with a little corn he'd carried behind the saddle. He gave Rio some meat, peas and a dried dumpling he'd saved from the supper he'd had in Polson.

He sat on his saddle in the bower and, munching on a biscuit, wondered if Larris Jule was still at the cabin. He wondered how much further he'd travel before getting back at his pursuers.

Throughout the night, the icy snow

continued to fall. He drank another cup of coffee and pulled the saddle blanket over his head. Twice he crawled out shivering and stoked up the fire. Then it got so cold and so near to dawn he stayed on his feet, stamping them for feeling.

A fresh blanket of snow covered any tracks he'd made. Up to this point, if Jule's men hadn't seen his fire or its smoke, they'd have a hard job following him. Again, he wondered if he should wait and make a stand or go looking for them. They wouldn't be expecting that. But he thought it best to keep moving until something happened.

When eventually day came he made more scalding coffee. Then he warmed the mule's blanket over the remains of the fire and packed his traps.

He moved off into the white, soft world. The mule did have sound, reliable footing and Will rode what he estimated to be ten miles. They continued east, but were pushed further north by the terrain. He rode for hours through stands of spruce and aspen. Near midday Rio caught himself a pocket gopher, but Will and the mule made do with the contents of a can of peaches.

Late afternoon, Will rode down into a gully, then up to a shallow, sloping plateau. The land then fell away into rough, ridged territory that stretched dead north. He figured that if he carried on riding, it would eventually bring him to the headwaters of the Swan River; the land where he'd usually spend his winters, trapping wolves.

Along the ridges, the timber was old, first-growth pine. The air was blue-shadowed and very still. He held to the crests of the ridges as long as possible then dropped cautiously into snow-filled ravines, crossed and rose to the next ridge. Will knew that if he kept going north then bent west, he'd get near to Polson within a week. If he swung south, he'd be on his own land and challenging Jule again.

Near sunset, the night winds started to surge off the mountains. Will swore at the cold, started off into a brown study. He'd been riding with a memory of Linny Jule, and it got stronger as the darkness grew. She was standing outside of his cabin, her eyes fixed on him. Her pa needed her support but she was torn between them. Will had just about everything going for him, except the side of her nature that wouldn't allow a killing.

Will was holding the reins lightly, walking the mule when without warning it flung up its head, dragging him from the saddle. He grasped the reins with his free hand, leaned out and went to ground.

'It's all right, it's only a hole,' he reassured the alarmed animal as he got to his feet. 'A few hundred feet deep maybe, but only the width o' your gut across. We can step it. Rio! he called out with a calm he didn't feel. 'You follow on. We'll show you how it's done.'

Will didn't waste any time. He pulled

on the mule's bridle, inched it forward until its hoofs struck the ravine's edge. The animal gave out a harsh blast from its nose and throat and Will let the pressure off for a moment. 'Come on, stretch your neck. You're already halfway across,' he said. Then he pulled sharply on the reins again.

Suddenly one of the mule's hind feet slipped. In panic it lunged forward, its momentum carrying it clear across the gaping hole. The movement caught Will off balance, but still clinging to the reins he pushed himself out and landed beside the mule. He was dragged off his feet again as the mule sought stable footing, got to his feet and put a hand on the animal's trembling neck. 'I wasn't goin' to jump. I just thought you'd like to know,' he said, wryly.

Will's face was sticky and when he took off his hat, sweat ran through his stubbly face, left salt on his lips. Cautiously, he led the mule downward, away from the ledge. 'We ain't god-damn lemmin's,' he greeted Rio as the hound went snuffling past them. 'You're supposed to be on the lookout for things likely to kill us.'

The trail he was on descended through icy shale to the brink of a creek far below. By the time they got there, the mule was dead beat and Will stopped at the water's edge to unsaddle it and put on a loose hobble. He did without a fire, just rolled in his blanket again, with Rio close up for the comfort. Most parts of him ached, but sleep caught him before he felt the pain in his bones.

★ ★ ★

Some time after Will had made the jump, Lester Madge and a man called Goober York halted their horses. They'd cut the tracks of Will's mule as it left the trail along the canyon floor.

'We'll wait here for the others,' Madge said.

Two hours later, it was Larris Jule who arrived with Tom Moss, a hired gunman. York told them of the loss of two riders.

'Stryker must think he's on a goddamn buffler shoot,' Jule snarled, rubbed at the pain high in his shoulder. When he'd simmered down, it was four men again who pushed uptrail. They followed Will's clear prints until darkness caught them on the switchback.

York suggested they retreat to better ground for night camp. 'We'll over-ride the place, smudge up his tracks with ours, won't see where he turns off,' he reasoned.

Jule got down from his horse and led it forward up the switchback. 'Where's he supposed to turn off?' he sneered and continued on towards the top of the ridge.

'We're tired, an' so are the horses. Why don't we make camp, have ourselves some grub,' York complained.

Jule kneeled and lit a match a few inches off the ground. He took a close look, walked forward and stared into the darkness, then came back. 'Stryker's goin' on. He's pushin' for the high ground,' he told them.

'Goober may be right. The feller could break trail anytime,' Madge said.

'Well if he does manage it, he'll ride west for a time. He was serious about takin' us one by one. So if he don't, he'll be wantin' to get back to Polson. He could head for the ranch even, to finish it there. I would, if I were him.'

Jule led them forward, and every hundred yards or so he dismounted and flared up another match. It was late when they neared the rim of the canyon, where he eventually found Will's prints. He dropped the match, stamped on it quickly.

'Down there. He's below us now. Let's move,' he directed his men excitedly.

'I reckon not,' York objected. 'That's a one-time Bole Mines track. They had burros to take 'em up an' down to the cabins. We go now, get stuck halfway down, how'd we get back? That's if we don't fall to our deaths before.'

'Stryker made it down, goddammit,' Jule snapped.

'That was by daylight, Larris. An' besides, he's got *us* on his tail,' Madge put in.

The whites of Jule's eyes smouldered eerily in the darkness and his voice got shrill. 'I can almost sniff him. He ain't more'n two hours ahead. We go.'

'I know this land, you don't,' York continued his grumble. 'There's breaks in the trails, I'm tellin' you. We're still a spit out o' Bole, so I ain't for playin' up like a bighorn.'

'If Stryker's still alive, he'll still be there in the mornin', Madge said coolly.

Jule stood thinking for a moment. Like most inherently fearful men he sensed some relief in holding over. 'I already sent a man into Bole. But someone goes back downgrade to watch the creek. Stryker could make a trail through there, get back around us. You know the country, Goober. You go,' he ordered.

12

Cold Trail

Will watched the first, bleak veins of light seep into the canyon. He sat up and shuddered inside his blanket, worked at the aches in his back and shoulders. He smoked a string of cigarettes and waited, got to thinking that if he'd left Linny Jule to freeze, up in the Snowshoe country, he wouldn't be in such a dire position now.

Then he noticed the mule had strayed. He looked upstream, saw that the animal had moved against its hobble, had started to nose at some waterside vetch. He quickly got to his feet and ran forward to keep the mule and the vetch separated, looked beyond the mule to the dark, blocky shape of a miner's cabin.

The place looked deserted but,

drawing the Remington, he went forward tensely. Watching for movement, listening for the merest sound, he pushed a boot against the part-open door.

Inside the old, tar-boarded place, he saw very little, the vestige of a double bunk along one wall. 'Fair fixins',' he muttered, thinking of his own poor night's lodging, then went back to bring up the mule. With a weird survival instinct, he turned to look back along the creek bed. A hundred yards away, a man suddenly hunkered down. Goober York was sited on a big, oval boulder, and he brought a rifle sharply to his shoulder. He fired, and the bullet spat and whined off rocks less than a yard from where Will was standing.

The mule flung up its head at the sound and Will made a run for it with Rio, mocking the excitement with a bark. Will pulled the hobble loose, and ran the mule back towards the cabin. Another bullet chopped up the ground ahead of him and another shattered a plank of the cabin wall. Will slung the fetter rope around the mule's neck, heaved it through the doorway. Then, with Rio close at heel, he made one more return dash to grab back his saddle and blanket.

The marksman was firing systematically as Will swung the saddle across the mule's back. 'They found us, all right,' he called out to Rio, as more lead smashed up the cabin. 'We're goin' to have to get the hell out o' here.'

The excited hound leaped on to the remains of the top bunk, and Will drew the mule as far back as he could into a corner. He swore with gusto as he watched the black clapboards disintegrate, the floor inside the doorway erupt with grey, dusty puffs.

Then the firing ceased.

'Hah, that'll be his reload,' Will said, 'The bastard'll probably move now.'

The day started to open, and the creek trail grew brighter. Will knew that a chance shot would soon reach him, cripple the mule or Rio.

He stepped to the small, side window and tried to see along the creek, but the angle of view was too narrow. He edged around to the door, pulled off his hat and peered along the creek. The rifleman was contemplating what to do next, had the barrel of his gun dipped. Will swore and ducked back quickly, wondered how many of them were out there.

'What the hell we done to deserve this?' he shouted, as he chugged the mule back out through the door.

He was more than forty feet downstream by the time York fired off two more shots. He held in close to the edge of the canyon wall, risked a quick look back. York was kneeling, going for a steady, more accurate shot. A moment later the bullet scuttled the shale at the mule's feet, close to the water's edge. Will ran with the long curve of the wall, until a minute later he looked back again, saw that he was screened by the ascending rock.

He stopped and saw that across the

fast-running creek, the ridge wall fell in heavy folds of rock and timber. It was a rough slope, but passable. He put the mule into the water, and at once he heard the renewal of gunfire. He turned against the current for better footing, felt the current surge hard against the mule's legs. A bullet zipped into the water close by, and the mule lurched forward. It regained its balance and moved on again, stepped onto the stony bankside. The timber ran down close to the water and Will shouted for them to gain shelter. They quickly reached the trees and Will swung down, pulled the carbine from its saddle holster.

He leaned into the trunk of a spruce, held the shortened barrel of his carbine in the fork of a low branch. He considered the distance and drew a thoughtful sight on where he estimated the rifleman to be. He let out his breath, took up the trigger's slack when York appeared in the distance. It was an easily missable shot, but Will saw its effect as the report of the carbine echoed sharply between the walls of the canyon. Back along the creek, the stalking rifleman jerked sideways, pulled back and down out of sight.

Will took a breather, sat down with his back against the tree. He knew that, out of sheer cussedness, Larris Jule would give him no rest. 'That'll learn you to keep your head down for a while,' he muttered, indicating that Rio stay still. He guessed that the pursuing men had split up, and that Jule would probably be coming at him from above. He'd have to make a move now, head south-west, back towards his ranch and Polson.

Knowing the rifleman along the creek wouldn't choose to make a target of himself, Will holstered the carbine and walked them out of the trees, moved carefully along the shallow, dipping side of the creek. For a quarter mile, the track opened up and he picked his way through the overgrown debris of Bole's played out mine workings.

After an hour, Will recognized the high shoulder of the entrance to Box

Canyon. He'd be east of Post Creek, almost back to square one with a good eighteen miles of cold riding on to Polson. Five or six hours if he was lucky, scary time if he wasn't.

The wind was from the north, the sky was slate grey and augured more heavy snow, possibly a norther. His mule was a good one though, and knew its way over snow and icy trails. But by noon, Will doubted if he'd travelled more than five miles. Several times he'd taken shelter in thick stands of timber to avoid the first, hard-flurried snow. When they reached Bole Creek, he cracked the thin, pearly shell of surface ice to water the mule.

The bitter wind was howling down the canyon from its northern end. It burned Will's face and deadened his fingers. It was late dusk when he eventually emerged from the maw of the canyon, rode into the thinning stands of spruce and aspen. He called in the hound, looked incredulously to the town that was holed up ahead of them.

13

Creek Diggings

Bole didn't have a street. Blue wood-smoke curled from ramshackle buildings, and in the last light of the day, lamps glowed yellow from a lone, grease joint saloon.

The garbage can town was now only a stopping place for drifters, for the badmen who found places like Polson, too busy. A handful of prospectors worked barren digging holes at the fag-end of the Bole Creek strip. They were tight-lipped men, accustomed to the wilderness and Bole's distinctive brand of whiskey.

Will dismounted outside a weathered skeletal structure that was the livery. 'What's the charge for puttin' up a mule?' he shouted from the open doorway.

There was a surge of coughing before a scrawny man carrying a lantern came limping from the shadows. 'Them that asks is usually runnin' from some sort o' trouble,' he rattled, during a searching look at Will. 'If a mount needs corn, it needs corn. That's what I figure.'

'I'm not runnin'. I'm lookin' for someone.'

'I got no memory for that sort o' thing, pilgrim.'

Will tried a different tack. 'I own a ranch west o' here. Name's Stryker. You heard o' *me* perhaps?'

'Hmm.' Then the stableman spat. 'If I was to believe what *some* folk got to say around here, Stryker's the feller who *don't* own a ranch.'

Will took a quick step forward. He grabbed the man and dragged him up close. 'Listen, wood foot,' he threatened. 'If someone's been talkin', tell me, or I'll shoot your other leg off. You hear?'

The man blinked hard. 'Take it easy,

pilgrim,' he croaked. 'He's in the saloon. Ain't left the place since he rode in.'

'What's he look like, this long lingerin' man?' Will asked.

'Heavy, got a small head. He's a queer-lookin' cove. Don't let a smile crack his face. If I was you, I'd be thinkin' o' clearin' town.'

'You ain't me. An' you're goin' to put my mule up an' give it a bellyful o' corn.' With that, Will walked back to the door. He bent his head against the wind and made his way to the saloon.

Butty's Stand was a twelve-foot run of split lodgepole sided to a single room. One man had his elbows on the counter, talking to the barkeep. The man with the small head sat alone at one of three tables. The three men looked up when Will came in. Seeing he was a stranger, the barkeep took a closer look.

An untouched platter of cold greasy steaks lay on the counter. Another offered hard soda-biscuits and small onions. Will moved to one side.

'Whiskey,' he said, 'or whatever you call it here.'

The barkeep's eyes narrowed for a moment, then he nodded and poured the drink.

'Jesus,' Will rasped, as the firewater hit the back of his throat. Then he turned slowly, looked at the man at the table. 'My name's Will Stryker,' he said flatly. 'You the guy with news regardin' the occupancy o' my ranch?'

A muscle quickly tugged at the corner of the man's bloodshot eye. He was in a bit of trouble, wasn't expecting the prod. He sucked air through his teeth at Will's goading. 'Was just chewin' the dog, Stryker. I normally keep out o' business that ain't mine,' he said with practised menace, trying to make some time.

The man looked directly at Will. He knew the look of a man who wasn't troubled much by killing, knew that if he drew his gun, it wouldn't be clear of the table top before he died.

'Both hands on the table, an' ease yourself up,' Will told him. 'I promised Jule I'd get my ranch back. Said I'd take him an' his men out, one by one. *That's* the mistake you made, mister . . . bein' one of 'em. Now, get out o' that chair.'

The man was another who was hired by Jule for his gun, and now he could hardly believe what was happening. He was going to have his chance to use it, more than an even break. He'd claim the $100 and a share of the sale he'd been promised. Slowly he pushed the chair backwards, unbent his girth from the table.

He rolled his eyes up, but it was too late to see Will's punch coming. He wasn't set to take a punch, and he was way off balance when the blow caught him below his right eye. White light exploded, turned to dark inside his head. Curious, dull sounds came and went, and the next moment he was on the floor.

There was a sour taste in his mouth

and he dragged himself into a kneeling position. His breathing was fast and shallow. He was wondering what to do next, when Will's hands gripped at the lapels of his tight-fitting coat. He felt his bulk being heaved up, then the sudden, dull shock as his broad back and shoulders got slammed hard into the wall of the saloon. His head bounced forward and he threw an arm out in front of him. He was now breathless, and he tried to focus, take a bearing on Will. His instinct was for hanging in, and he tried to reach his gun. It was his trade, and he'd always relied upon that ability as a first and last resort. But it was too late.

Will's bunched fist caught him hard in the mouth. He tasted blood and came off the wall swinging, took a wicked blow in his belly. He lost all his remaining wind, got doubled up to Will's lifting knee that smashed his nose.

'You listen good, mister,' Will said kneeling beside the man. 'This really ain't your sort o' business. Now you been saddle broke, I suggest you ride north before winter sets in. Move any further west o' here, an I'll take it to mean you're lookin' for me. An' Mr Jule will tell you, that ain't to be recommended.'

Will got to his feet, threw a weary, disgusted look at the barkeep. 'If *he* forgets what happened here, make sure *you* tell that goddamn Jule when he arrives,' he snapped. Then he turned on his heel and walked out through the door, whistled for Rio to join him.

A minute later, Will returned. At the bar he used a neck cloth to wrap up the steaks and biscuits. 'Never leave meat in the doghouse,' he advised the barkeep wryly, and tossed a coin on the empty platter.

14

One Night

Goober York sat glaring at Larris Jule. 'He could've taken my goddamn head off along that creek,' he complained of Will Stryker's gun shot along the creek. 'Why don't we get on to the ranch, lie up for him there? We know it's where he's headed.'

'Eventually, yeah. Polson's more likely for what he's got in mind right now.'

'That's a long, wretched mile from here,' Lester Madge put in.

'How far?' Jule asked of York.

'I'd say five hours. Four, if we keep goin', which I ain't in favour of.'

'No, I can see you wouldn't be. What's the matter with you?'

'I got a real bad pain in my chest. Feels like I got caught under a log boat.

Pill pusher in Washin'ton State said it's a heart condition.'

'That's a great time for one o' them,' Jule said, with a pitiless shake of his head. 'How far are we from Bole?'

'Another hour, why?'

'I told you, I sent a gun there,' Jule explained. 'If he'd met Stryker he'd have rode back to tell us. He'd have to come this way.'

'So we go into Bole an' find out,' York reasoned. 'Get us some grub. They might even've lit a fire.'

'No. We go straight to Polson.'

Madge sat his horse, unmoving. 'An' what if Stryker was there?' he asked. 'Think about it, Larris. A few hours here or there, don't really matter. We got to ease up. Maybe Goober can get himself some physic.'

'One night,' Jule conceded summarily.

★　★　★

The barkeep was staring at the ceiling when Jule, Madge, Goober York and

117

Tom Moss pushed their way in to Butty's Stand. He lowered his eyes and cursed at the icy draught, moved a greasy bottle along the counter.

The four men looked with distaste at the candle-lit contents of the back bar.

'You got one o' them spittin' cans?' Jule asked.

'Why?' the barmen asked, with little concern.

'I'm guessin' it's where the contents o' this bottle's goin' to end up.'

For a moment the barman thought about Jule's insinuation. 'Use the floor like everyone else,' he suggested. 'Watch out for folks' boots though. Some o' these old grubstakers can still cut up rough.'

Jule had already noticed that all three tables were occupied by prospectors; hostile men who spent more time in the saloon than at their worked-out digging holes. 'I'm lookin' for someone. Kind o' meaty, carries a gun, an' a head that don't rightly fit,' he said. 'You'd have seen him in here.'

'Yeah, he was here,' the barman said straight off. 'But now, he's carryin' a bust-up head.'

'What d'you mean?'

'There was another feller came in — wore a sawed-off carbine strapped to his leg. He didn't have need of it though. He used his fists to beat the frost out o' the man you're lookin' for. He left a message for *you*, if you're Jule.'

'I'm Jule. What message?' Jule asked, chary of the answer.

The barman worked his face into a mean grin. 'Well, it was more of a warnin'. He said for you, *not to go west*. If it was my business, mister, I'd be takin' heed.'

While Jule pondered the second-hand threat, York asked the barman if the town had a doctor.

'Not for much more'n staggers, we ain't. You sickenin' for somethin'?'

'Never mind,' York answered, and grimaced as he swallowed the searing liquor.

Jule reached for the whiskey bottle, had a closer look at the label. 'This feller with the long gun?' he asked, pouring York another glassful. 'He happen to mention where he was headed?'

The barman shrugged. 'I got the feelin', him an his dog don't want no one lookin' for 'em.'

Jule snatched off his hat. Sweat broke out in a thin line across his forehead, and wild, extreme rage showed in his eyes. 'I'm not interested in your goddamn feelin's,' he snarled. 'I was askin' where he was headed, you goddamn piss pusher.'

'He never *said* where he was headed.' The barman suddenly saw the dangerous, volatile nature of Jule, looked circumspectly at Lester Madge and Moss. 'But even if he rides to first light, he won't get no further'n Polson,' he added less belligerently. 'There's a squall pickin' up from the mountains. Goin' to be a real fence-downer.' The barman didn't like anything about

Larris Jule. He thought better of mentioning Will Stryker's promises about getting his ranch back, taking out Jule and his men, one by one. He smiled at the wicked thought. 'You could ask at the livery,' he suggested. 'Riders tend to mention where they've been. Now and again, where they're goin'.'

'I doubt Stryker's one o' *them*,' Jule returned with a bilious look. He turned to consider the rumble of the disquiet miners, their suspicious, challenging stares. One of them gave a long snort, another spat dark juice from deep within his whiskers.

'You set for fixin' us some grub?' Jule asked the barman tersely.

'Sorry, mister, not at this hour. I could fix you another round, before you leave.'

Madge sneered, 'Reckon he wants rid of us, Larris.'

'Not before we pay him, he don't.'

York held up his hand. 'I can't take any more. I already got a mule inside o' me. This liquor's got it kickin' my ribs out.'

'That ain't no mule, Goober,' Madge contributed. 'It's what they're purveyin' as whiskey, in this stinkin' dump. What do *you* say, Larris?'

For a response, Jule looked to the barman. 'You got a couple o' rooms on top o' here?' he asked.

'Yeah. Four dollars before you go up . . . fire damage an' breakages when you come down.'

'You remember that gopher hole called Whitefish, we passed through, Larris?' Madge grinned. 'Them beds was already burnin' when we fell into 'em.'

Jule gave an indifferent nod. 'I'll take 'em,' he said. 'We're stayin' the night.'

'One night? What about your friend here?' the barman asked of Jule about York. Jule looked around him as though for a fitting place to spit. 'Why, he'll most likely be dead by mornin',' he spluttered.

The barman struck a match. He lit a fat candle that was wax-welded to the counter, wondered if someone would grasp the meaning. 'Then this'll be for you . . . shortly after,' he muttered.

15

Forking Out

Will had told Larris Jule that somehow, he'd despatch him and his men. And Jule wasn't a man likely to heed the barman's reminder of that promise either. If anything, it would further madden him, spur him on to a more reckless pursuit in the direction of Polson, back to Will's ranch. But Will was a man who kept his word, or at least tried to, so he wasn't leaving Bole just yet.

The livery was the place to stay low. Jule would be back for his paint and the three other horses, so Will could make up his mind from there, have another crack at shortening the odds. He'd already got some satisfaction in beating a Jule gunman with his fists, and he expected another opportunity.

His knuckles still stung a bit from the skull thumping. But if they didn't all come for their horses, he wouldn't be firing off his carbine.

For a dollar he'd spent the night beneath the haymow, wrapped in a horse blanket. The ground was damp and it stank of old dust, manure and straw. He'd used a pile of empty sacks as bedding, and at his feet, Rio was persistently troubled by the bite of hardy mites. Even knowing it wasn't for much longer, didn't make the rank, chilly hours any easier to get through.

Just before first light, the interior of the livery was in its usual heavy gloom. An overhanging lamp was still lit, but no one had yet stirred. Staring at the rough-hewn crossbeams over his head, he waited for several minutes, but there was no sound other than the stableman who coughed and slept in his cot sill above the grain bins. He got to his feet and looked out at the yard. Ice was sheeting the water trough, and a cat stepped neatly through the spokes of a wagon wheel.

There was a rear door, narrow and low, but it was another way out, he noted cautiously. From far off, a timber wolf howled, emphasized the bleakness. He listened to the horses munching grain, the occasional stamp or snort. He moved back beneath the overhanging haymow to wait, let everything get used to the notion of him not being there.

He'd got the timing just about right, didn't have too long to wait. Tom Moss had come to collect the horses, would be leading them back to the saloon.

Will moved slightly as Moss unhurriedly turned into the livery. He felt something touch his shoulder and he put his hand up, touched a bridle and bit that was hanging from a wooden peg. He waited a few seconds, but the man was alone. He gripped the bit firmly but carefully, to prevent any noise. Then he eased it from the nail, and in one smooth movement tossed it underhand, towards Moss.

The iron bit clanked into a pile of

empty cans. 'You tryin' to be funny, Madge?' the startled man called out. 'Now you're here, stop messin' an' gimme a hand with this tack.' For a second or two, the man's words hung in the oppressive silence. 'I said, stop messin', Lester,' he went on, a trace more uncertain. 'This ain't exactly a commandin' situation we're in.'

Will was carrying the carbine in his left hand. Raising the barrel, he took a step forward. 'You can say that again, feller,' he said. 'Now that ain't funny, an' I ain't your Madge.'

Moss stepped away from the horse he was looking to saddle, 'I got three dollars even,' he replied, after a nervy moment assessing Will. 'That'll buy you the price of hot water an' soap, a bed for the night, an' a drink if you're startin' early,' he added unpleasantly. 'Now, you goin' to use that long shooter, or is it just to frighten me?'

'I ain't goin' to waste a bullet on you, you sonofabitch. I already used a handful on them friends you've chose to ride with.'

The man groaned, as the thought struck him. 'Will Stryker.'

'Yeah, the man with a crow to pluck.'

Moss took a close look at Will, his eyes flicking to the carbine. 'Me an' York had a wager on whether you'd been here,' he said. 'Jule wanted to press on to Polson. Madge reckoned a few hours here or there, didn't really matter. Ha! It seems it did.'

Will drew back the hammer of the carbine with the ball of his thumb. 'As long as Jule persists in goin' for my ranch, I'm always goin' to be somewhere,' he advised the man. 'That goes for the henchmen he's payin', too.'

Fear suddenly shadowed Moss's features. 'So far you been real clever, leadin' us on a chase through these goddamn mountains. But you fire that thing, an' all the vultures get a peck at their quarry,' he said, and shuffled his feet, backed off a half step.

Will jabbed the carbine. 'Right now,

128

it's you got to worry about what he does next.'

More perturbed by Will's purpose, Moss looked around him. 'You ain't got that knobhead saddled,' he observed.

'What makes you think I'm leavin'?' Will retorted.

The man gave a thin, wily smile. 'You ain't goin' to risk dyin' in this muck pile. An' you ain't goin' to shoot me in cold blood, either.'

'That's right,' Will agreed. 'I already told you, I ain't wastin' a bullet on you.' With that, he let the carbine fall to the floor, and he moved his right arm from behind him. 'But you're still gettin' some holes in you,' he explained, sliding his hand nearer the twin tines of a pitch fork. 'Didn't you know that trouble never comes single-handed?'

'You're goin' up against me with *that*?' the gunman sneered.

Will shook his head. 'Not unless I have to. My old hound's about to fall from the rafters an' bite your nose off,' he grinned disturbingly.

Moss knew of the red tick coon hound, had seen him in the mountain snow. His mouth twisted open, and for an instant he was suckered, then his hand moved fast for his Colt.

Will was aware of that, though. It was his advantage. His arm muscles were sprung and ready before his antagonist made the move. It was a solid, powerful movement that sent the fork, chest high, across the stable.

The long, sharp prongs found their victim. They went in deep, trapped the man's wrist, his gun hand, hard against his ribs. He moved his other hand, but did nothing more than make a rigid grip on the handle. The stabbing was fast and final. There was nothing could be done for him, and he knew it, as he waited for the pain.

When it surged through his body, Moss didn't make much of it, Will gave him that. A sharp intake of breath, then a strangled, coughing curse, was about all. The sudden chill, the darkness, the wretchedness of dying, the man went through it all without a sound. He dropped his Colt, but remained standing, licked at the blood that seeped from the corner of his mouth. His eyes bored through Will, as if he was expecting help to come rushing through the open door. But no one came, and he fell sideways into the stableman's empty peach and tomato cans.

Will picked up his carbine, took a few short steps across the stable. 'You're another o' Jule's gunmen that really ain't worthy o' their hire,' he said. 'Why'd you do it?'

The dying man turned his head towards Will. 'Same as the others. A hundred dollars.'

'I wonder what he'd have paid a true specialist,' Will said, with unbelieving contempt. 'Crazy thing is, I reckon I'd have let you go, if you'd have asked.'

'I wouldn't have done that,' Moss said. Then he closed his eyes against the white fire that ripped through his insides, the overwhelming silence.

'I know it,' Will said curtly.

He thought of Jule, wondered how he was going to deal with the man who was still Linny's father, wished it was all over.

'Hey, Rio. We got to go now,' he said reassuringly. 'Whether them that's left, chooses to die's up to them. If they do, it'll be in Polson. Then we go home. I promise.'

Rio scuttled down the short haymow ladder. It was where he'd gone to escape the mite bites.

Will dragged Moss's body to the rear of the stable. He wasn't going to take out the fork, so he lay the dead man on his back. Then he piled his bedding sacks and some dirty straw on top, close around the bloodied, clutching fingers. 'It won't be the smell that gives you away,' he mumbled, looked up to where he knew the stableman had been silently watching.

He saw the man's eyes glisten from his cot. 'Won't be long before they come lookin'. So get down here an' find somewhere to hide this stiff's horse,' he

132

rasped. 'But you say one word to 'em about what happened, an' I'll come back an' plant you alongside him. You hear me, old feller?'

16

Dead Beat

Avoiding a direct route to Polson, Will moved into the foothills. He was going to make a loop from Bole, follow on to the route he knew his adversaries would be taking.

For nearly a mile, he traversed the broken ground of a dry-bed creek. There were walls of rock to either side, and occasional island boulders to negotiate the mule around. Rio would drop from in front to behind. He'd flush out a quail, send it flapping noisily through the trees, then he'd run around to lead again. When the eastern wall broke down to a gap, Will made his way out through the gnarled roots of creekside timber. He took them to a point where he could view the land east of Box Canyon, where three riders made their way along a corded ridge *en route* to Polson and the ranch. It was as he thought: Jule hadn't wasted any time on rising to the threat of moving west.

Will continued on a course through the snow-covered timberline, turned now and again to look at the dark peaks of the Missions. From now on he'd keep to the rim, that he might keep better watch on Jule's party. If they got strung out, he'd likely get a shot at whoever brought up the rear, make a better number for the inevitable gun fight they were all heading for.

Near to midday, Will looked again at the western approaches to the canyon. He saw that Jule's party was now riding to the base of the ridge. Without dismounting, he watched the riders wend their way to where the evergreen timber broke on to the flats. When he was certain that Polson was the objective, he started downgrade, worked his sure-foot through the scree to a point where he'd get near to crossing them.

An hour later Will had closed on the group. He dismounted, scuffed up some lichen for the mule to snatch at. From now on, he was going to stay in reach, bide his time. Snowflakes were in a heavy, plumb fall, and he held Rio against his chest for reassurance and warmth, waited patiently until the sound of a brief exchange came to him.

It was Goober York cursing the cold, the going, the fact of being there. Rio met Will's eyes, for ten minutes waited brightly for a sign of direction. But only when the outfit had swung away, did he move to sniff at the cold air.

Head down, Will rode quiet and cautious until he cut Jule's trail. They weren't far ahead; he could take one, maybe two of them well before they reached the flats or Polson, even. But if things went wrong, it wouldn't be *him* telling the tale. He flicked the snow from the brim of his hat and followed on patiently.

The terrain became less broken and the timber started to thin out. The trail bent further west, dropped away from the long mountain slopes. Another hour of pursuit and Will saw hoof prints that were sharper in the carpet of fresh snow.

He halted a mile above the timberline. If he followed on they'd see him. Now, they were less than a two-hour ride from Polson, and they'd shoot him from the saddle. He decided to stay in cover and smoke some cigarettes, then ride further north, before bending back. It wasn't going to matter to Jule either way. To him, it was the end of the line, whether Will was in town or on the way there.

Will was walking the mule slowly, was brushing a snow-loaded branch aside when he saw Rio drop to a crouch. The dog's tail flicked sharply, brushed at the snow in warning. Then ahead, Will saw the horse. Beside it, a man crouched on both knees. Beneath a wool blanket, his arms were clutched tight around his ribs.

The man turned his head as Will

approached. He made a feeble effort to reach his Colt, but his hand just dropped away. Will didn't bother to pull his carbine, because he was looking at the man's face. The skin was grey around dark lips, and he was sickly sweating, despite the cold. Will knew he was in the company of one of Larris Jule's men.

He climbed from the mule, pushed the man's horse aside. 'Do I know you, mister?' he asked.

The man hardly raised his eyes to Will. 'Not exactly. We exchanged a shot or two. Goddamm ticker's givin' up on me. I knew it would . . . been warned. Should've gone back,' the man growled huskily.

'What's your name?'

'York.'

'They left you here, York? Larris Jule gone an' left you to die, has he?'

'They're in a hurry.'

'A hurry for what?'

Goober York was breathing shallow. 'To get you box fitted,' he murmured.

He lifted his head, squinted hard at the man he'd had in his rifle sights along Bole Creek. 'What you think I can do for this goddamn pain?'

'You got to be some sort o' dumb-ass askin' *me*. Why the hell d'you think you're up here?' But Will found a few dry branches, some bark and duff to get a fire going. It was small, but sheltered by the low ground and the aspen. 'No way I could've rode off with you feelin' the chill an' all,' he said without sentiment.

The man's eyes held an ill-fated bead on him. 'You found Jule's guns, didn't you?' he accused. 'Back in Bole. Jule reckoned Tom Moss run out on us.'

'Yeah, I found 'em. But we never exchanged names, an' neither of 'em run out on you . . . not exactly.' Will shivered, looked east towards the crushing cloud.

'How long before it hits us?' York asked.

'There ain't no 'us', mister, an' you'll be floatin' long before first light.'

139

York stifled a raw cough. 'Jule never told us about the rime that covers you, Stryker. He said you'd got stuff belongs to him. Said you'd see it that way, an' skedaddle back north.'

'What do the others say?'

'There ain't any others, an' you know it. Jule really ain't got much help any more. Madge stays 'cause you shot his kin.'

'Your paymaster's a real bad judge o' character, ain't he?' Will sneered. 'Never knew a man who got it wrong, just about every time.'

'You'll send somebody back?' York despaired in a cracked voice.

'Yeah,' Will lied. 'Like you would for me.' Then he called for the hound, turned back to his mule and remounted. The two remaining men didn't amount to significant odds, he considered, and he'd settle on an encounter in Polson. He hoped that being near home gave him the edge, and that with the diminishing returns of his manpower, Jule would be the one to get his nerves racked. It's why he left no sign of the gunman, Moss. For an absurd moment, Will deliberated on the man cutting and running back to the Flatheads.

Thirty minutes on, and the mountain trail ended. Out on the flats, between himself and where he sat the mule, the snow swirled near the ground, as if to shirk the oncoming norther. 'We come some sort o' full circle, boys,' Will acknowledged. He could hear eerie groans in the distance, the cracks and grindings as the shifting ice waters from Bole and Post Creeks gathered their force. The big, fearsome innards of the storm was hours away yet, but Larris Jule and Lester Madge wouldn't be far-off from Polson.

Rio yipped, gave an outstretched leap, as if he wanted a saddle ride. 'Yeah, this sure ain't no gully-washer,' Will commiserated. 'But it won't take us on this night. It'll clear for a while, then wait till early mornin' . . . catch us in our beds.'

If there had been a sun, it would have fallen long west of Polson, when they set off after Jule. Will looked down at Rio. 'We're goin' to make for the bench south o' the canyon. There's higher ground there.' He understood Rio's nervy side, that he'd run from the weather that was going to hit them. 'You ain't goin' to like it,' he explained considerately. 'An' it ain't your sort o' fight either. Why not go back to the timber, an' bite some rabbits. Go on! Me an' the mule'll get us beds in town.'

17

Whiteout

A messenger wind was pressing down from high Mission ridges. The first Canada geese were returning from the south, and Will watched them, followed their flight across the face of the moon. Then the clouds darkened, and he shivered, turned the mule through the chilly slush into the gloom of the livery.

'Caddo!' he called out. 'The men I came lookin' for a while back. You seen any of 'em again? They been here?'

Emerging from the refuge of his small, stove-heated room, Caddo drew his scattergun from the mugginess of his fur robe. 'Yep,' he granted, indicated Larris Jule's paint mare that was standing back in the stable shadows. 'Got a pack dog with him.' The livery man slanted his eyes at Will. 'The girl brought my buggy back. I reckon she's still in town if'n you're interested.'

Will nodded. 'I'm goin' to be. Meantime, I'll be availin' myself o' that byre o' yours for a few hours,' he said. 'No need to tell you what you'll suffer, if that gets out.'

'Same as last time. You'll set fire to me,' Caddo mumbled, as he drew his face back inside his scarf.

Will climbed tiredly from the mule. 'Not if I've got Jule's bullets in me, I won't,' he responded with little humour. 'If you got any windows, keep 'em shut. This town's gettin' drowned, before a full night's out, an' it won't waste time in comin'.'

He'd known full well that Jule would be laid up in one of the few buildings that had a view of the lodging house. With no scruples about using his daughter as a lure, the man would be waiting for his quarry. With Lester Madge in attendance, there'd be little hope of ferreting him out.

So, Will took into account the extent

of his backing. He didn't think Abe Dancer would be of much help. Under the fast-approaching blizzard, the town's sheriff would be making sure his family were out of harm's way, most likely trade a street patrol for the relative safety of the hotel bar. He considered the whereabouts of Buckham Sendaro, wondered if he'd be out setting beaver traps, if he'd be stalwart in a gunfight.

Will toe'd the door in to the lean-to. Holding the carbine down at his side, he lay flat on his back on the cot, closed his eyes and set himself to wondering. There'd be an opportunity before long. The squall would meld with the ice-flood to find a natural route into town. With it would come an adequate distraction for his next move.

He woke under the torrential deluge, grey light leaching through the swollen, splintered walls of the lean-to. He stood for a moment listening to the explosion of hail on the livery's grain shed. His thoughts centred again on Linny, her predicament within the lodging house. He was reasonably certain that nothing much had moved during the night, and nobody was going far now.

★   ★   ★

For the long hour of a slow-breaking dawn, Linny had been sitting by a side window of the lodging house. Deeply disturbed, she watched the overpowering shadows move from the mountains. She knew about snow and ice storms, the unimaginable destructive power when ice-bound headwaters broke from high ground. As the full rage of the whiteout rolled over Polson, icy shards struck, gushed at the window glass until there was nothing to see. Linny wondered on Will Stryker's confrontation with her father, but turned away before establishing an outcome.

She drew a slicker from her carpet bag, pulled on a slouch hat and made a move to the front of the house. She took a deep breath before pulling open the door to the street, recoiled from the onrush of frozen air. The low-lying street was already overflowing, the rising water shoving branches and broken ice along its turbulent course.

Linny hung to the step rails, watched a teamster untying a mule from a mud-trapped ore wagon. Some folk stood in their doorways simply staring at the flood, others ran here and there for no plain purpose. At one of the two stores, a man and a woman had dragged provision sacks into the doorway. Their boy swung from a support rail, laughing, kicking his foot out at the swirling water.

Linny ran back through the lodging house to the rear door. The steps descended to the edge of the swelling water and she jumped down, made it safely to the raised gallery of the other store. A woman and two small children were huddled inside, their faces showing the first unmistakable signs of panic. The man stood further back talking to a prudent Abe Dancer.

'What are you doing to help? Shouldn't you be out there, advising them to get out of town,' Linny demanded breathlessly.

'They don't need advisin',' the sheriff answered quickly. 'They ain't bundlin' up for a potlatch. There's a limit to how the law can help in these circumstances.'

Linny shook her head with distress, felt the knot of frustration deep inside her. She looked to the shopkeeper and his family, knew there wasn't much of a future in reasoning.

Further along the street, almost at the limit of Linny's vision, somebody was pulling at the gate of the livestock pen. 'There's enough water backed up from them goddamn creeks to wash us to Missoula,' he was yelling. 'We all got to get out o' here.'

Linny guessed that most townsfolk had already made it to the south side of the street. She had a last imploring look at those around her, then decided to attempt the lodging house again before getting away.

Immediately she was in racing water, with fragments of torn-out building planks swirling around her ankles. Through the hiss and blow of the storm, she heard the strains of shifting support timbers, then a first ominous rumble from the mountains. She stopped for a moment and dropped her shoulders, tried to keep her teeth from rattling with the fear. Up in the Flatheads, there was an immense yearly snow melt that swelled Snowshoe Creek. But south of the big lake, something more deadly heralded spring. A big, bad, blue norther was choosing the moment when incalculable tons of freeze water surged from high in the Missions.

Linny changed her mind about going back. Survival was more important than any travelling fumadiddle. She started to run south and east of the town's buildings, wanted to catch up with the other folk who were heading for the higher benches below the timberline.

But she'd left it too long, and the racing torrent pressed hard at the back of her legs. Off balance, she fell, gasped as the chill smacked at her body. She lifted her face, dragged numbed fingers across her mouth and blinked her eyes. She staggered upright, and lurched on. She'd lost her hat now, and her slicker had come open. She could see the shape of her body through the flat, sodden folds of her dress, tried vainly to refasten a button.

Her breathing was difficult and she was sobbing with despair when she stumbled and fell again. But this time, there was a foot pressing into the small of her back. Somebody held her down for a long moment, before drawing her upright.

'Shouldn't be out in this weather, missy. Could come to real harm,' a voice rasped nastily.

Linny twisted to face the man who'd spoken, but that was all. Lester Madge's broad maul of a hand clasped tight around her face.

18

Hell of a Day

Will was now some distance from the livery. He was standing beneath the overhang of Sentence Hotel when the squall hurled itself across town. The clouds blacked out much of the light that overhung the rush of flood water, and through the icy flakes that whipped his face, it was as much as he could do to see halfway along the street.

He'd seen something like this spectacle of nature only once before, was acutely aware of the danger. The mighty head of water would follow the land contour that led from Lonepine Lake, then seek the broad, low-lying path into Polson. Will knew where Linny should be; his problem was getting there without getting himself killed or endangering her. There wasn't much time, and she might have fled already.

He swore and walked full into the blizzard, hurried between buildings that were already encircled with swirling currents. He drew the carbine from its long holster, and shouted at some frightened horses that had been scattered from the pen. Further on, the proprietor of Beers and Spirits was securing four beer kegs outside of his saloon. Will hadn't forgotten Jule and Madge, and gave a hard glance. 'Hell of a day,' he said, getting a look at the man's troubled face.

The roaring was oppressively louder by the time Will fought his way to the rear of the lodging. He looked up, but couldn't see any windows of the building, guessed that if she was in there, Linny wouldn't be seeing him either. Across the deepening torrent, he threw himself for the step rail, pulled himself up to the narrow door which was swinging on its hinges. A deep, rolling roar from the east meant the flood water was escaping the confines of the Missions.

'Where *are* you bastards?' Will yelled, his nerves jangling. He expected a volley of bullets every time he flung open a door of the deserted building. On the second floor he found one that was locked and called Linny's name. He took a step back, hit it with the heel of his boot and it crashed open.

He pointed the carbine down at the single bed where Linny was lying. She'd been gagged and bound, abandoned by her captors. He shoved the carbine into the knot behind her back and drew her up and into his body. 'Just think of it as dancin',' he rasped, as he edged them out through the room door and on to the short landing. 'I'll get us out o' here,' he promised rashly as they made it down the stairs, as the first surge of big water reached them. The building moved enough to make him stumble, almost fall to the ground floor. Then the backup swell hit low against the walls. The foundations shifted, the floor beams groaned and windows cracked.

Will pressed his back to a slanting side wall at the front of the building. He pulled the carbine from Linny's bonds, eased the gag from her mouth. 'You all right?' he asked, having noticed she was wet through. 'This stuff'll rust your stomach, if you swallow too much of it, you know.'

'I was supposed to be safe here. You *said*,' Linny gasped.

'I never did,' Will responded with a tight smile. 'You must've got the wrong idea, an' for that I'm real sorry. I know your pa's in town, Linny. You ain't goin' to tell me it was *him*, who did this?'

'Lester Madge. I guess it's the same thing. Now you've gone and sprung their trap, Will.'

'Yeah I know it. Took a bait I couldn't resist. I guess that's what you done to me.'

For a moment their fingers held, as Will teased the binding from Linny's wrists. 'They're somewhere's out there, watchin' an' waitin',' he said. 'With this blow an' all, we're in one hell of a scrape.'

Linny was near to tears. 'All this comes with owning a ranch, does it?' she asked tiredly.

'No. It all comes with tryin' to hang on to it.' Will kneeled to free her ankles, saw the water seeping through the puncheoned floorboards. The building slewed underfoot, then canted from level, as a corner stanchion gave way.

'But we got options,' he offered, with a calm smile. 'Drown, or have the building collapse on top of us. *Both*, if we don't get out o' here.' Will said it, knowing that supporting Linny would cut his fighting chances when they got outside.

'It'll take more than a hog-tie to stop me,' she said, with feigned pluck.

Will had a quick look around them, decided the rear door was still the best bet. The couple worked their way along the sloping floor as the house twisted again. A long gash opened beneath their feet, and icy dirt water sluiced in. The door was partly open, but jammed, warped tight shut against its frame. Will cursed and pointed to an adjacent side window. He knocked out the remains of a broken pane. 'Don't want that slicin' us up,' he mumbled, and rammed up the sash.

The scene outside stunned him. The town had its footings gripped in a whirling rushing flow of water. Some of the smaller buildings had already subsided, others were creating breakwaters for timberline debris. Drifting around the lodging house, Will could see sluice and cabin timbers, battered tool crates that had rafted all the way from the worked-out Bole Mines. Among young spruce and old pine, the dark fur of a coon glistened, all locked together in the throes of drowning. There was nothing but the frosted water race between where Will and Linny were trapped, and where bales of hay floated free from Caddo's livery at the south end of town.

The snow was still sleeting down

156

thick and heavy, but for all its might and phenomenal drama, Will thought the flood wasn't worsening, not getting higher or faster in its flow. 'Hey, it ain't goin' to get any worse,' he yelled, above the groan of the pitching building. 'It's nearly done. From now on, it'll drain out into the range.'

Will's attention then switched to the whereabouts of Larris Jule and Lester Madge. He knew they had to be watching from somewhere. *I'm* here, because I'm supposed to be, he was thinking. An' *they'll* most likely shoot me dead, the moment I leave.

Linny shared the thought. She was shaking with fear as she looked at Will. 'You're not going to tell me to stay, are you? Not again.'

'Hell no. You got to paddle us down to Missoula,' Will told her. He considered a swift grin, but noted the panicky tremor in Linny's voice. 'I'm thinkin' there's another reason you ain't keen on stayin',' he added. 'Somethin' you ain't told me.'

Linny nodded. 'Madge threatened me. He said, there'd be a price to pay if . . . '

Will didn't need Linny to finish Lester Madge's threat. 'We ain't *all* deservin' of our kin, Linny,' he said, with a concerned shake of his head. 'Your pa's runnin' with maggots, an' that's a fact.'

19

Shaky Town

From having clambered out to the top of the rear steps, Will saw what was stopping the lodging house from further collapse. It was pitching on to a floating jam of wood sheds and bin stores.

'Home ground ain't lookin' too rich. But the water ain't risin' any,' he said, taking his carbine from Linny. 'Still deep enough for the bath I been plannin' though,' he mused, just above a whisper.

'We've got to get out of here, Will,' Linny said, easing herself through the window space.

'We're of a like mind there, Linny. We'll make our way up to the benches. That's where the others will have gone. I'm hopin' that old Caddo's got my mule with him. I ain't for wastin' ten dollars.'

For a moment, Will stared at the stark flotsam, wondered if the body of Goober York would arrive, dead, swimming through the icy waters. Then he looked through the snowfall to the town's remaining structures, flinched at the thought of the first bullet from Jule or Madge. 'So let's go,' he shouted.

* * *

South-east of Polson, high above the water race, Will and Linny mingled with the wretched dispossessed. They were silent people, huddled close in their distress. They'd lost just about everything, save their hefty clothing and some blankets. Occasionally, Will called for Rio. He had a feeling the coon hound was down from higher in the timberline, was probably making up his mind how near to get to the wet trouble.

They found Caddo, and he'd found

the buggy and got it harnessed to the mule. Linny was going to busy herself with comforting, try and soothe the heartbreak and tears, not least her own. It was a way of dealing with Will's purpose in going back. She kept reminding herself of what he'd said about undeserved kin, thought it was all so unfair. She was going to ask him what he'd do, decided that he'd do what was needed. And that would be best, because now she loved him. She gave a curious, quick smile.

'What was that for?' Will asked.

'You. You remind me of Dan Tucker.'

'Who's he?'

'He's in the song; 'Old Dan Tucker went to town, ridin' a mule leadin' a houn' . . . ' Doesn't it remind *you* of someone?'

'No. I won't be takin' either of 'em.' Will returned the smile, only for longer.

With a solitary purpose, Will turned from the benches, back towards the shattered town. He knew that neither Jule or Madge would lose time in getting shot of Polson, if they'd witnessed the lodging house going down. But it wasn't, so they'd still be there.

Far to the north of the town, his eye caught a flicker of movement. It was a mounted figure who fluttered in and out of vision in the thick swirl of snowflakes. Who the hell's *that*? he wondered, before whoever it was, was lost again to the vast, white landscape.

Will actioned the carbine, blew snowflakes from around the hammer, small heat on to his fingers. As he approached the wrecked remains of the livestock pens, he plainly saw that beneath the crusting of broken ice, and although still running knee-high deep, the flood water had started to slow and subside. But the town of Polson wouldn't be standing in the same way again. It ain't all bad then, he thought wryly. Perhaps next time they'll get 'emselves a town planner, or the like, get things built somewhere up near the benches.

He watched for signs of movement among the stark remains, a glint of gun barrel from atop a deserted building. 'Where the hell are you?' he hissed.

The few walkways and porches that were annexed to buildings, had been swept away, and those that retained a foundation, were enterable. Some of the more hardy folk had remained, were already estimating on the salvage, Will supposed. He made his way in and around the rear of the south side buildings until he came to the Sentence Hotel.

The building was holding together, but the downstairs windows were all twisted and broken from their frames. He glanced inside, saw that the bar room was now a mud-swathed surface beneath tables and chairs, bottles and glasses. There were no footprints to show the place had been entered since the rising water had surged in. 'Not in here then,' he muttered, flexed his taut fingers on the grip of the carbine.

Will turned away, glanced across the

broad swirl of water to the office of the Circuit Sheriff. The place was single-storey and block built, was protected either side by stone cells. He half expected Abe Dancer to appear through the mud-splattered doorway. Instead, Jule and Madge elbowed their way on to the stoop, their faces grim with hurtful purpose.

20

Break Up

Will took a deep breath, wondered if he'd done something real bad in a previous life. But he wasn't one for superstitions, so he cursed the men's livers.

'Sheriff ain't at home,' Jule shouted into the blasting wind.

'An' you surely ain't got the posse,' Madge added.

The two men were out of reliable range for their Colts. But Will didn't want to provoke too soon, and remained very still. With the carbine, he could drop one, maybe both of them from where he stood.

But Madge knew, was reasonably certain, it would be him first. Will assumed the goading was rash settle-ment for the death of the man's nephew. Then Madge said something to the effect, and it was Jule's expression that gave the game away. That was reason enough for Will to make his move.

Madge had regained some self-control though. He'd moved behind Jule, shrewdly stepped back into the office by the time Will had levelled his carbine.

'Gunfighters shouldn't let sentiment get the better of 'em, Madge,' Will yelled. 'It'll lead to places they oughtn't to be.' He aimed low, shot twice at Jule's legs.

Jule made a sharp, jig-like jump, drew his Colt and fired back at Will. But the bullets were way off their mark, sliced their way high and wide into the solid backdrop of snow.

Will took a deep icy breath and brought up the carbine for a more considered shot. 'No more kickin' heels or dogs, for you, daddy hogdirt,' he rasped, seeing a leg shatter below the man's knee.

As Jule fell, he clutched an overhang support, fired again, this time closer to Will's body.

Will cursed and fired again, a final frightener into the hanging sign above the stricken man's head.

But Jule was finished. Screaming, he went down to the hefty boards that skirted the front of the sheriff's office. Will looked away from him, saw the blur of a figure running low from the building beyond one of the cells. It was Madge, and he'd be making for the rear door of the saloon. More like a practised gunman, he'd try and get close, go for a side-swipe as Will exchanged gunfire with Jule.

'You're leadin' *me* then,' Will proposed acidly.

On reaching the rear of Sentence Hotel, Madge fired twice. Will snorted wearily and snapped off a shot in return, hurled himself sideways to cover.

With his back pressed hard against the wall of the hotel, Will paused to reload and listen. There was no sound, save the cursing groans from Jule. He guessed that Madge had found the rear door, was probably in the sleeping shed, and hearing the same. He took a few cautious paces, stopped beside the half-open front door. 'Jule's finished, Madge,' he shouted. 'Like me, you ain't got no real need to die. It's up to you.'

Then Will heard another sound from above him. He looked up, saw a run of clapboards bulge, felt the door frame shift beneath his fingers. 'Goddamn buildin's on the move.' he muttered. He pushed the carbine around the door, took a step into the muggy chill of the bar room.

Almost immediately, Madge's gun roared and the lintel of the door frame shattered. But Will didn't go back. He hurled himself forward and down to the floor. A shadow passed across the glass-fronted door to the rear room and it clattered as it slammed to. Madge was now falling back, waiting for Will to follow him in.

Will eased himself to his knees. He kept his eyes on the door in front of him, got to his feet and edged towards the bar. Over his head, a happy jack lantern swayed as bearing timbers moved again, and the blizzard started to whistle through breaches in the clapboards. Will stood very still for a long minute, until he saw the shadow again. It was a slow, dull movement behind the door, and he thought he knew what it meant. Silently the handle turned, and Will hunkered to the floor. With his carbine held across his chest, he eased himself behind the bar, where the murky, narrow confines reeked of mud and stale liquor.

21

Drowning Rats

Lester Madge was in no hurry to get the connecting door open. He wasn't certain, was hoping that his shot had forced Will back outside of the building.

But Will was going to wait it out, wait his chance like the coachwhip. Then, dark scufflings among the piled glasses and bottles on the shelf that ran alongside his shoulder caught his attention and he twitched.

As Madge came through the door, one, two, then a third rat dropped onto Will's shoulder, and ran down his front. They'd been hiding up under the bar, a refuge from the swirling torrent of water that had flooded their creepy runs.

The bile rose and Will's heart hammered. His throat constricted and he recoiled in mute terror as tiny claws scuffed across the fingers of his gun hand. The rats scampered to the floor around his feet, and he couldn't hold his position any longer. He was forced into going for Madge.

'Meet the whole goddamn family!' he yelled in defiance, and rolled out from the shelter of the bar.

Madge spun on his heel and found Will with his Colt. 'Kid Killer,' he bellowed back and pulled the trigger. The blast was still resounding madly around the walls of the bar room, when Will fired again.

Madge's bullet had punched into the sodden floor inches from Will's face. His second just missed because Will had rolled frantically to one side.

Will fired again, and knew that was it. 'Reckon right's on my side, if God ain't,' he rasped.

Madge faltered as he got off another round, as his legs buckled. But Will had moved again, taken another full spin away from the bar. He knew it would be the end if he made it so, and he was leaving nothing to chance. As Madge's bullet hit him in his left side, he extended his right arm. At what seemed to be point blank range, he fired up at the man's dazed features.

'You made it to your grave, Madge,' he said, as above them, low roof beams cracked loudly from their trusses.

With bullets in his belly and chest, Madge collapsed alongside Will. Will twisted around to look at him, for a few moments lay very still. With the exhaustion of relief, he listened to Madge's gulpy breath, and inched closer.

'It ain't much to do with God or bein' right, Stryker,' the man said hoarsely. 'You win 'cause the likes o' me an' young Slender got no place of our own. You do . . . that's the difference . . . the difference *you* live for. I guess I should've told the boy about homesteads.'

Will nodded. 'It might've helped,' he agreed tiredly.

Madge grimaced hopelessly and lifted his chin, then his hand from the floor. He squeezed the Colt's trigger one more time, and something burst in a spout of gore and fur. 'An' I hate rats,' he gasped and closed his eyes.

Will dragged himself back to his feet, as all around him the walls of the hotel groaned. The front of the building bulged again, but this time it couldn't be contained. It broke away, sent a great billowing cloud of snow ahead of it. Then, like some big-jawed raptor, the roof folded in.

With one hand pressing against the wound in his side, Will backed through the warped doorway. Then, leaving the saloon's vermin to nose the bloodied corpse of Madge, he half fell, half jumped to the swell of ice and mud below him.

Wincing at the surge of pain, he dragged himself further away as the building went into a remarkable corkscrew motion. It collapsed into an isle of timber, and Lester Madge's tomb floated off to merge with the rest of Polson's flotsam.

It signalled an end to Will. He was suddenly aware of the lonesomeness and desolation, and his knees recognized it. He looked around him, north towards where he'd first seen the figure through the snowstorm. But the man was a lot nearer now. Riding a big, winter mare, he approached from the direction of the lodging house. The wind snatched at his fur robe, for a moment, revealed the crimson tunic of Sergeant Ashley Cameron as he raised his hand in greeting.

Will thought of Linny, and cursed. 'The bastard's come to get her. Or me,' he rasped miserably.

22

Starting Over

'Still killin' folk I see, Stryker,' Cameron called out as he rode close.

'You ain't seen nothin',' Will retorted. 'Fellers just drop dead in these parts.'

'With .45 carbine bullets in 'em, I'll wager.'

'Well I'm carryin' lead too, in case you ain't noticed. You rode more'n a hundred miles to keep an eye on me?'

'No. You really ain't that important,' the mountie countered with a dutiful smile. 'It's Larris Jule I've been trailin'. He was gettin' to make *too* fast an' fat a profit on the saddle brokes. Most o' the last delivery were runnin' into the corrals, still wild. I'm purchaser for the border forts, an' accountable. It's to *me*, he was sellin'. Them miles ain't much when it's a personal matter.'

'Yeah, I really do understand. I was thinkin' o' leavin' him. But seein' as you're here now, an' he's your captive, you can save him. You want to see Linny?'

'For what? Tell her I'm takin' her pa back to the Mcleod Prison Infirmary. I don't think so. An' he'll freeze solid if he's left out here for much longer. I'll patch him up, get him to a doc in Kalispell.' The mountie turned his horse away, then checked and looked back. 'Nearly forgot,' he called out. 'Up along the loggin' camps, a couple o' tinhorns been tellin' a tale. They're sayin' it was Joel Beeker up to his ol' gamblin' tricks aboard the Flyer. Seems he pulled a gun on a feller when he shouldn't — got himself shot dead because of it. Means, the RCMP murder indictment's been dropped.'

Will stared with surprise at the mountie. 'If ever I meet up with *that feller*, I'll pass it on,' he responded drily.

It was a strange procession that straggled north-east from where Polson now remained, broken and desolate. Through the bleak, white landscape, a motley collection of wagons, hand-carts and buggies were strung out behind Will Stryker and Linny Jule.

The townsfolk brought with them salvaged essentials; bread and molasses, tinned fruit, milk and tomatoes. On the three to four-hour journey, they drank coffee and spruce tea. The animals went hungry or ate corn from what nosebags Caddo had managed to drag from the livery stable. Will's coon hound ran back to the head of the line, dropped a well-chomped hare at the feet of the mule, panted its pleasure on returning.

For an hour, Will and Linny hadn't spoken much, merely listened to the sounds of grim travel, the animals' hoofs and wagon wheels as they crunched through the snow and mushy ice.

'What do you think will happen to Pa?' Linny eventually asked.

Will stepped his mule closer. 'You know, I *really* don't much care, Linny,' he said. 'I know he's livin', which is more'n he had in mind for me. I'm sure the good sergeant will find somethin' fittin'.' He grimaced at the heave of pain in his side, looked behind at the bedraggled trail of men and women, the small number of children. 'It's *them* I'm thinkin' of right now.'

Linny nodded her support. 'Me too,' she agreed. 'They truly are a lawless society now. That's why they're looking to you. You can at least show them how to survive, which is a lot more than the law's able.'

'Yeah, well, it ain't quite the same as huntin' wolf. Where we're goin', there ain't even a cookshack. I got me a cabin an' a corral, a shed with firewood, an' that's it. They'll have to go back an' start over . . . rebuild the town.' Will gave a quick mischievous grin. 'Or move on down to Missoula, seein' as

178

their homes an' businesses have gone on ahead of 'em.'

'That's not funny, Will. They've lost everything.'

'I know that. An' when we've all ate what few head o' cattle's been left *me*, I'll be joinin' 'em. I ain't no long-term poor house.'

It was five more thoughtful minutes, before either of them spoke again.

'I never did thank you for rescuing me from the lodging, did I? I guess I'd be in a pretty wretched state by now,' Linny said.

'Whatever the state, it was always goin' to be a pretty one. Savin' you from the misfortunes of frostbite, seems like a fine habit for me to get into,' Will flattered. 'Perhaps even big, bad, blue northers have a silver linin'.'

Linny smiled agreeably. 'Tell me about Canada . . . what you wanted up there,' she said.

'Well, I ain't responsible for no unlawful deaths. I *never did* murder anyone, if that's what you mean.'

'I didn't . . . don't. I wanted to know what you wanted there. I'm assuming there's a difference.'

Will smiled at the recall of Linny's pernickety way. 'Yeah, there is. I went up to buy me a couple o' Milk River bulls. I found out the Canadian Pacific was payin' top wages for rock splittin' out on the Calgary loop. Thought I could use the extra dollars to buy some line breeders at the big, border pens. They'd have been a real stock improver.'

'And what was it stopped you?' Linny persisted.

'I had a ticket on the Flyer. Made the mistake of sittin' in with a bad crew, though. One particular jasper didn't like my way o' winnin'. I certainly didn't like his.'

'Which was?'

'*I* had Jack Spade headin' up a runnin' flush, an' he had a belly gun. We had a short argument.'

'An engaging defence to take into a court-room,' Linny replied. 'I get the general idea though.'

'What else do you want to know about me?' was Will's question.

'How'd you get that scar on your hand?' she asked, without pausing.

'His name was Spike, an' I tried to take a bone away from him. It was a long time ago.'

The snow started to ease off, and a brighter sky opened up across northern Montana. It was a full quarter-hour later, before Will continued.

'The geese are back, so green-up shouldn't be more'n a few weeks off.' he said. 'I could start over. I earned that money. It's in a loggers' bank in Kalispell.'

A twist of doubt flitted across Linny's face, and she shook her head. 'I know someone who could use a fair-minded horse dealer. And Caddo's looking after the paint. Like me, it won't be harbouring fond memories of Snowshoe Creek.'

Will pondered for a moment, then looked pleased when he got the picture.

'Horse breedin' ain't my work though. I'd need help.'

'Well, I need to earn my keep, and I *do* know horses,' Linny offered.

Rio suddenly barked, went off ahead, lumbering through the drifted snow.

'We're nearly there, an' I think he remembers,' Will said. Then he gave Linny a quizzical look.

'What are you thinking now?' she asked.

'Who was it, led his gang to the Promised Land?'

'That would have been Moses. And they were his *people*, Will.'

'Oh! Weren't your Dan Tucker then?' he said and grinned.

23

One More Gun

'I'm sure that Ashley Cameron really is keeping an eye on you, Will,' Linny said.

'Why'd you say that, knowin' he's halfway back to Fort Mcleod?'

'Because he's not. He's up there . . . been watching us for nigh on an hour.'

From the doorway of his cabin, Will looked to the east. It was where the timber ran along a snow-covered ridge. 'That ain't the good sergeant, god-damnit,' he said after a long look. Then his voice became a hard whisper. 'I reckon it's someone who *ain't* rode north, someone who ain't took hard warnin'.'

Linny's voice immediately held concern. 'What do you mean, Will?' she

183

asked. 'Please don't tell me we've got more trouble.'

'Probably not,' he lied. 'I'm guessin' it's a travellin' man, lookin' us over. Maybe he's got some bitters or quinine. I'll ride up an' take a look.' Will saw Rio respond to the word 'go'. 'Sorry, feller. Can't take the risk o' you scarin' off our caller.'

Linny knew that something was wrong. She clutched her hands, looked at Will in obvious distress.

'Look for my signal. I'll be back soon after you see it,' he said confidently.

* * *

From the cabin, Will turned the mule south, as if making for the wagon road. Then he rode a tight loop west, then north into the timberline. It was only an hour from first dark and he didn't want to lose his quarry in the shadows of the close timber. If a watcher atop the ridge had wished to kill from ambush, he'd have his horse close, probably in a

184

scoop where snow drifted.

Ahead of him, his lookout magpies rose up, and a rabbit flashed its scut into tunnelled cover. The wind whipped through the light snowfall, stirred the tops of the trees where he dismounted. He grinned with resolve, lifted his boots through the thick carpet of snow.

Now and again, branches dropped their snowlines, and Will flinched at the silent movement. He circled to the knoll where he'd seen the figure of the waiting man. There were no tracks and Will guessed he was right about the horse being tethered below the ridge. As he got closer he held in tight to the trees, listened for a give-away sound as he blinked against some gusting snowflakes. He stepped over a gnarled root spread, saw the horse below him in the snow-packed hollow. It was a dun mare that stood waiting, head down and disconsolate.

Will moved closer slowly, merged with the blackness of the stark, upright trees. It was darker now, and the birds had moved their roost. The cold started to bite, and Will flexed his fingers around the carbine, raised the barrel to hip level. He'd wait for the failing light to merge the shadows, then make a move if he had to.

But within a few minutes the horse snorted and shuffled. Flailing a Winchester at the snow-covered branches, the man was coming back from his vantage point, and Will gritted his teeth.

The heavy, small-headed gunman moved from the cover of the timber, had a sudden, cautious look around him before reaching for his saddle holster.

'You don't frighten easy then?' Will rapped out.

The man gasped and swung his rifle in a short arc. A blade of flame stabbed at the gloom and Will jerked backwards. He felt the shock as the bullet thumped the tree beside him, as his neck caught a splinter of bark.

'Perhaps this'll worry you more,' he yelled. He hunkered and fired, realizing as he did so, that the gunman was still a fast and practised shot.

As if in acknowledgement of Will's thinking, the man took a short step away from the dun, and fired again.

'Mistake!' Will rasped.

The man shook his head, realized he'd lost his cover as Will's bullet hit him high in the chest.

Will rolled to one side. He pulled himself into the bole of the tree, and waited. He wasn't about to reveal himself to a man who'd suddenly become dangerously wounded. He listened to the chatter of his teeth and the grate of his breathing, the snorting of the frightened dun.

Time drew on, and Will waited, worried now that the first man to make a move was going to be the first to die. 'Christ, the cold's most likely killed him,' he muttered after another full minute. He got to his feet and came out from behind the tree. The horse glared at him and backed off, strained at its bridle tether. 'Easy, girl. No more shootin',' he said. He walked forward, prodded the body with the carbine. Nothing moved and he grabbed at the man's coat, rolled him face up. He saw the warped mouth, the facial damage that he'd meted out to the gunman with his own fists.

I told him to ride north. Must be one of 'em that keeps comin' back, he thought. Another one who wouldn't be claimin' any $100 an' a share of the sale he'd been promised. He considered hauling the man up and across the saddle, thought better of it. Instead, he untied the length of rope that was tethering the dun mare. 'I'm goin' to have work for you,' he said. 'Meantime, come an' get acquainted with my mule.'

Ten minutes later, he walked close to where the gunman had waited earlier in the day. In the distance, and to the west, amidst the night blue landscape he saw the yellow glow from a string of hanging lamps.

'That's tellin' me to come home,' he said. He pulled off his mackinaw and pushed it into the low branch of a tree. He struck a match and held it to the oiled wool, stood back and watched the flare up. 'An' *that's* to let you know I'll be there,' he added.

THE END

WEST OF EDEN

Mike Stall

Marshal Jack Adams was tired of people shooting at him. So when the kid came into town sporting a two-gun rig and out to make his reputation — at Adams' expense — it was time to turn in his star and buy that horse ranch he'd dreamed about in the Eden Valley. It looked peaceful, but the valley was on the verge of a range-war and there was only one man to stop it. So Adams pinned on a star again and started shooting back — with a vengeance!

BAR 10 GUNSMOKE

Boyd Cassidy

As always, Bar 10 rancher Gene Adams responded to a plea for help, taking Johnny Puma and Tomahawk. They headed into Mexico to help their friend Don Miguel Garcia. But they were walking into a trap laid by the outlaw known as Lucifer. When the Bar 10 riders arrived at Garcia's ranch, Johnny was cut down in a hail of bullets. Adams and Tomahawk thunder into action to take on Lucifer and his gang. But will they survive the outlaws' hot lead?

THE FRONTIERSMEN

Elliot Conway

Major Philip Gaunt and his former batman, Naik Alif Khan, veterans of dozens of skirmishes on British India's north-west frontier, are fighting the wild and dangerous land of northern Mexico. Aided by 'Buckskin' Carlson, a newly reformed drunk, they are hunting down Mexican bandidos who murdered the major's sister. But it proves to be a dangerous trail. Death by knife and gun is never far away. Will they finally deliver cold justice to the bandidos?

A BULLET FOR MISS ROSE

Scott Dingley

In the aftermath of a bank robbery in Terlingua, Rose Morrison lies dead. Assigned to pursue her killer, Ranger Parker Burden learns that the chief suspect is the son of his friend, Don Vicente Hernandez. Teamed with a Pinkerton detective, Parker pursues Angel Hernandez to Mexico, shadowed by bounty hunters. They become mixed up with the tyrannical General Ortega and uncover a sinister conspiracy. There is a bloody showdown, but has Parker found the one who fired the fatal bullet at Miss Rose?